"What are you running from?" Barely a whisper, Will's question floated to her.

Silence stretched between them.

Annie tipped her head back against the seat. Running? The man thought he had all the answers. This time he was much too close to the truth. "Will," she pleaded.

"Okay, you're right. Now isn't the time." He let out a breath. "I'm sorry."

"I'll say you are," she said, taking a light tone again. "One sorry Sullivan."

"Hey, I'm trying to apologize here."

"You don't need to apologize to me. Keep shooting straight. I count on that from you. Give me a few days. Let me rest, clear my mind and sharpen my wits, then we can have this conversation. Deal?"

"Always have to have the last word."

She opened her mouth to protest, then clamped her lips shut.

Will laughed.

The sound warmed her like a quilt as her gaze found the May moon.

TINA RADCLIFFE

has been dreaming and scribbling for years. Originally from western New York State, she left home for a tour of duty with the Army Security Agency stationed in Augsburg, Germany, and ended up in Tulsa, Oklahoma. While living in Tulsa she spent ten years as a Certified Oncology R.N. A former library cataloguer, she now works for a large mail-order pharmacy. Tina currently resides in the foothills of Colorado where she writes heartwarming romance.

The Rancher's Reunion
Tina Radcliffe

Steeple Hill®

Published by Steeple Hill Books™

STEEPLE HILL BOOKS

Steeple
Hill®

Recycling programs
for this product may
not exist in your area.

ISBN-13: 978-0-373-81525-8

THE RANCHER'S REUNION

Copyright © 2011 by Tina M. Radcliffe

www.SteepleHill.com

Printed in U.S.A.

Take thereof no thought for the morrow:
for the morrow shall take thought
of the things of itself.
                    —*Matthew* 6:34

To my husband, Tom, my sister Anne, my parents,
Joseph and Teresa Russo, and to Tim, Mike, David
and Amy—thank you all for understanding this
writing thing of mine (or pretending to!).
I love you.

Acknowledgments

Thank you to my editor Melissa Endlich,
for helping me to become a better writer, and for
the wonderful opportunity to be part of the
Steeple Hill family.

To Meredith Bernstein,
thank you for your patience.

A final thank-you to my writing friends for their
support and encouragement: The Seekers
(www.seekerville.blogspot.com), Sharon Sala,
Jordan Dane (and the OKRWA Chapter),
and my longtime writing bud, Rogenna Brewer.

Chapter One

"You look awful." Will Sullivan shoved his hands into the back pockets of his Wranglers and continued his intense scrutiny.

"Well, you haven't changed a bit," Annie Harris said with a laugh. Leave it to Will to cut to the chase.

In truth, he hadn't changed. He was everything she remembered. Hatless today, his blue-black hair was clipped short to control the unruly curls. Will thought he could control everything. Standing inches over six feet tall in a faded blue oxford shirt, jeans and scuffed boots, he scowled.

Annie took an unsteady breath. Oh, how she had missed that scowl.

She gripped her cane tighter and glanced around the busy Tulsa airport. Had it really been two years? For only a second did she allow her thoughts to drift back to when she made the decision to leave for Kenya. The same day she realized she was in love with Will Sullivan.

"Sit down for a minute," Will said, interrupting her thoughts. "You've got to be exhausted."

"I'm okay. Really. The hospital wouldn't have okayed me to travel if I wasn't ready. Come on. Let's get my luggage and get out of here."

"Your leg? Maybe I should get a wheelchair?"

"Oh, I don't need a wheelchair." Determined, she grasped her cane and broke out in what she knew was a clumsy stride.

"Boy, you haven't changed much either, have you, Annie?" His long legs easily closed the distance between them. "Still think you have to do it all yourself."

Annie ignored the comment. She'd been traveling since she left Africa two days ago and was not prepared for a round of verbal sparring with Will.

They continued to walk down the large corridor until it forked. Annie stopped and rested her weight on her good leg while she read the signs overhead.

"This way." Will nodded to the right and walked in front, clearing a path in the hurried, late-afternoon crowds of the terminal. "Slow down," he admonished, as she caught up with him and began to take the lead.

She tried to accommodate, but her pace continued to increase, driving her. Excitement bubbled over. All she wanted was to get to Sullivan Ranch.

"So how was the flight?"

"Much too long." Looking around, she couldn't stop smiling. Her senses greedily feasted on the American sights and sounds. It was the simple things she'd missed; the twang of an Oklahoma accent, the U.S. flag hanging high in the terminal, a sign advertising Mazzio's pizza, the chatter of the crowd in English, and American food.

The tantalizing aroma of a bagel kiosk caused a pause in her steps. *Onion, chive and garlic.* They all called out to her.

"Want one?"

"I do. But not one. At least six."

"Six it is."

When Will stepped toward the kiosk, she laughed. "I'm kidding, Will. I don't want to eat anything until we get to the ranch."

"All right, but it's way past dinnertime, and you sure don't look like you need to be skipping any more meals."

"Are you calling me skinny?" She glanced down at herself. True, her clothes were a bit roomy, but she was alive and that was what really mattered.

"Turn sideways and you'll disappear."

"Someone is exaggerating." Looking up, she caught the amusement in Will's expression

"Not hardly," he said.

Annie held up her palm. "Okay. Truce? Just for tonight?"

"I suppose so. But that won't be much fun." He strode toward baggage claim.

Annie paused, taken back by his humor. The ever-stoical Will Sullivan had cultivated a sense of humor? Shaking her head, she followed him. "Is Rose at the house?"

"Are you kidding? Baking and cooking like crazy. She's got plans for you."

Annie smiled, knowing he wasn't exaggerating. Rose O'Shea was so much more than just the woman who ran the kitchen at Sullivan Ranch, and Annie couldn't wait to see her again.

Will stopped at the baggage carousel.

"Those are mine." She pointed to the well-worn tapestry bags.

"Got 'em." He easily hauled both bags off the moving conveyer as though they were empty. Hardly. Amazing how much she'd collected in two years. The rest of her belongings were shipped out in a trunk to arrive later.

With one bag under his arm, the other dangling from his hand, Will maneuvered out the automatic doors to the curb, where he parked the luggage.

Annie inhaled deeply. The springtime air smelled like rain. Everything was fresh and clean, exactly as she remembered.

"Wait here. I'll get the pickup."

"What? No. That's silly. I can walk."

He leveled his gaze on her but said nothing.

Too tired to argue, too tired to tell him not to get used to compliance, Annie simply eased herself to a bench and watched him cross the street to the hourly parking area.

A few minutes later a huge, gleaming black truck pulled to a stop next to the curb. Dark, tinted windows and spotless chrome glowed.

Will jumped out and picked up her bags, tossing them in the open flatbed.

"You bought a new truck?" She was more than surprised. Will never indulged.

"Life's short."

Life's short? Annie silently repeated the simple words to herself, the same words that had haunted her since the accident.

Finished with the luggage, Will stood straight and grinned, wiping an imaginary fleck of dirt off a shiny bumper. The expression on his face as he faced her was nothing less than pure male expectancy.

"That is one beautiful truck," Annie said.

He chuckled. "Good answer."

"What's that logo?"

"The Sullivan Ranch logo and URL. Brand-new. Like it?"

Her eyes widened. "Are you telling me you have a web page?"

Will gave a quick shrug. "Sullivan Ranch was taken, so I had to go with www.thesullivanranch. com."

"That means you have a computer."

"You bet. New laptop in my office."

Annie grappled with the concept of a modernized Will, while he opened the passenger door. She stared at the seat.

"What's the matter?"

"I'll need help to get up there."

"Turn around." He placed his hands around her waist and lifted.

The heat of embarrassment crept over her when he gently settled her onto the seat. "All r-right, th-then," she said.

Will walked to the other side of the truck and climbed in, apparently unaffected. "Sit back and relax," he said, as they pulled away from the curb.

"Yes, sir." She settled into the soft, smooth leather upholstery and released the breath she'd been holding.

Will smiled. "Tuckered out? Well, don't worry, after a little R & R you'll be back in tip-top shape, ordering right back at me."

"Promise?"

"Promise."

When a yawn slipped from her mouth, Annie leaned her head back, content not to think, hoping her mind would continue to cooperate and block the events of the past few weeks.

The silhouette of the familiar city faded as he led them out of town toward Granby, south of Tulsa.

What happened to the lights?

Annie searched in the dark, panicked. Suffocating fear clenched her body.

Another alert?

No, the antiseptic smells of the clinic were absent. She wasn't at the medical camp. Confused, she reached out and touched a warm arm. Her fingers automatically slipped down to the wrist to check the pulse. It beat strong and regular.

Annie blinked, eyes adjusting to the semi-darkness.

Will? Thank goodness, it's Will.

She was still in the cab of the pickup, which was now parked. The knot in her stomach relaxed then tensed again as Will's face inched closer, peering down.

"Hey, take it easy," he soothed.

"I'm fine."

"Yeah, sure you are. I've been trying to wake you for the past five minutes."

Annie scooted to a sitting position, wishing she could extricate herself from the awkward intimacy of the small space.

"I would have let you sleep, but I thought you might want to know when we got to the ranch."

"I do. I do. I've been waiting too long for this." Pushing back her hair, she crooked her neck to see past the dash to the sky. Burgundy streaks twined across the blue velvet, weaving themselves between the golden clouds of sunset.

Annie sighed. How many times over the past two years had she looked up at the night and paused, wondering what Will was doing in his part of the world?

"Looks like we're in for more rain," he commented.

"Red sky at night, sailors' delight."

Will scoffed. "I don't think so. Barometer's dropping. Weatherman says eighty percent chance of precipitation. Bit late in the season. I'm hoping he's wrong, but who knows? Might even get a good old-fashioned tornado for you."

Annie barely heard his response as her gaze took in the ranch's entrance arch framed by the Oklahoma night. The black wrought-iron gates stood proudly; "Sullivan Ranch" was spelled out across the top in black letters, with a distinctive letter *S*.

"You fixed the arch," Annie said, delighted at the sight. She had never seen anything more beautiful.

Will nodded.

"When?"

"'Bout a year ago."

"That long? It looks brand-new. Why didn't you write and tell me?"

"Why didn't you come home?" His answer was a low rumble that resonated through Annie.

"Now, Will, don't start that again." She knew the lecture by heart.

Will's mantra.

Home? Yes, it was Will's home, but she had no real right to call Sullivan Ranch home.

He bristled. "You didn't have to go halfway around the world to be a nurse."

"Are you questioning the call on my life?"

"No, but why is it when God opens a door you feel the need to run through the next three?"

Annie closed her eyes for a moment, regrouping.

His tone became gentle. "Rose has missed you, Annie. You know you're the daughter she never had."

What about you, *Will? Did you miss me?*

She couldn't ignore the frustration in his voice and countered with her own. "I know that, and I'm sorry. But Rose isn't always going to be around to pick me up and dust me off."

"That's just what I'm getting at. Rose isn't getting any younger." He rubbed his palm along his denim-clad thigh. "If you weren't happy at St. John's, why not work at another medical center in town? With the nursing shortage and all, you could have taken your pick." He continued without pause. "For the life of me I cannot figure you out. They're pulling Americans out of Kenyan refugee camps and you have to go in. Why can't you ever do anything the easy way?" His fingers clenched the leather steering wheel. "Where will it be next? Siberia?"

Annie turned and met his glance head-on. "I already checked. They don't have any openings in Siberia."

He stared at her for a moment, before the tension finally eased from his broad shoulders and the corners of his mouth pulled into a smile. "Keep it up, smart-mouth."

"Will, you have to do what you have to do, and I have to do what I have to do. It doesn't get any simpler than that."

"What are you running from?" Barely a whisper, his question floated to her.

Silence stretched between them.

Annie tipped her head back against the seat. Running? The man thought he had all the answers. This time he was much too close to the truth. "Will," she pleaded.

"Okay, you're right. Now isn't the time." He let out a breath. "I'm sorry."

"I'll say you are," she said, taking a light tone again. "One sorry Sullivan."

"Hey, I'm trying to apologize here."

"You don't need to apologize to me. Keep shooting straight. I count on that from you. Give me a few days. Let me rest, clear my mind and sharpen my wits, then we can have this conversation. Deal?"

"Always have to have the last word."

She opened her mouth to protest, then clamped her lips shut.

Will laughed.

The sound warmed her like a quilt as her gaze found the May moon. So many stars. Was the sky really clearer here? Were stars really brighter? She released a deep breath of contentment.

"Annie?"

When she turned her head their eyes met in the moonlit truck.

"I want you to know I'm proud of you."

She bowed her head, locking the words away to be savored later.

Will reached out and strong fingers gently pushed the hair back from her face. "You're wearing the earrings," he said, his voice a husky murmur.

Annie moved back imperceptibly; she wasn't strong enough to feign indifference to his touch. She reached up to finger the pearl studs.

They were a gift from Will her first Christmas at the ranch. She was only thirteen. It had been a bleak holiday for all of them. Will's first Christmas following his father's death. Annie's mother had recently dumped her with Rose before taking off yet again. It was just the three of them, and that was the way things stayed until Annie left for Africa.

"Yes. I hate flying," she replied.

"What?" Confusion played across his angular face.

"I wear your earrings when I need to be brave." She tried to laugh off the admission.

Blue eyes searched hers, before his hand dropped to her shoulder for a light squeeze.

Will looked up the road. He couldn't believe what he saw. The white clapboard farmhouse sat like a candle on the hill. "Rose has every single light on."

"Is she trying to tell you something?"

"Me? She wants everyone to know you're home. The woman is so excited and proud of you she can't stop telling everyone."

As the truck stopped Rose O'Shea burst through the front entrance, sending the screen door slamming against the house. Her gray topknot bobbed and the white apron around her ample waist flapped as she ran down the porch steps.

The passenger door was yanked open, and Annie slid out of the truck and into Rose's arms before Will could pull the parking brake.

"What on earth took you so long, Will? You stop for every squirrel in the road?"

"She made me go the long way." He lifted the suitcases from the flatbed and set them on the porch.

"I did not," Annie protested from within Rose's embrace. "He drove like an old woman trying to keep his truck clean."

Will watched Rose fuss over Annie, making clucking noises as she took the younger woman's face in her hands. "You've lost weight."

"Well, naturally," Annie said, stepping back. She gave a dismissive toss of her dark head. "Nobody cooks like you."

"How's that leg? Hurt much?" Rose questioned.

"No, it's more of a nuisance than anything." Annie stepped forward.

"Easy. Will, come and help her up the steps," Rose directed.

"Help?" He moved next to both women. "She bites my head off every time I try to help."

Before Annie could protest Will had scooped her up in his arms and started up the steps. He realized his mistake the minute she frantically wrapped her arms around his neck.

Annie Harris wasn't a scrawny little kid anymore. She might have lost a few pounds, but she felt exactly like a woman, with curves in all the right places.

Annie was a woman. Will stumbled at the realization. When he deposited her on the porch like a hot potato, she grabbed the railing for support.

The phone echoed from the house.

"That'll be my sister wanting to know if you're here yet." Rose flew past them.

"What did I tell you? It's just begun," Will said. He pulled open the screen door for Rose.

Annie still stood holding the rail, eyes wide and accusing. "That wasn't necessary," she said with a quiet voice. She yanked her pants and shirt straight and wouldn't look him in the eye.

"What?" he asked.

"Carrying me."

Her gaze flew to his, sparks of gold flashing in the dark eyes.

"Ah." Will took the opportunity to roll his shoulders in mock pain. "I think I pulled a muscle."

"You did not."

He looked her up and down and grinned. "Still a scrapper."

Years ago she'd stood on this same front porch, her hair in a single braid, enormous eyes staring. A little girl clutching a brown paper grocery sack which held all her belongings.

But Annie never cried. Not even when her momma left.

That was almost twelve years ago, the same day he set aside his own grief. At eighteen he'd recognized a soul mate in the brave kid who had been left on their doorstep.

He leaned back against the rail, his glance skipping over her. Long, silky chestnut hair flowed around her shoulders as she surveyed the land, a challenging tilt to her chin. Her brown eyes, almost gypsy-black, had dark smudges beneath them, telling signs of the ordeal in Kenya.

Will counted up the years. *Was she really twenty-four?* Twenty-five come winter. How did that happen? Hard to believe she'd be getting married someday.

Whoa.

Annie getting married?

He frowned. Was any man ready for Annie? He doubted the man existed who could match her toe-to-toe, heart-to-heart. The thought gave him an inexplicable satisfaction he chose to neither analyze nor explore.

Annie was a challenge all right, tall and proud, holding her thoughts locked deep inside. Pride was her middle name.

She'd tell you it was Elizabeth. Anne Elizabeth. He grinned, remembering how she had made it perfectly clear to everyone that she was *Miss* Anne *E.* Harris.

She turned to meet his gaze, hers questioning. "What's so funny?"

"Miss Anne E.," he said.

The corners of her mouth raised in a self-deprecatory salute. "Don't remind me." She pointed across the yard to a building in the distance. "What's that?"

"New stables. You still know how to ride?" he asked.

"I hope I do." Her smile deepened and she turned back to him. "How many horses?"

"Six, and quite a few boarders."

"The boarding has picked up?"

Will released his breath. "Not as much as I'd hoped." *Not as much as he needed.*

His eyes narrowed following her gaze as she looked out toward the orchard.

"Lots going on at the ranch, Annie. I've started a new business venture. This is the make-it-or-break-it year for Sullivan Ranch." He gripped the railing tightly with both hands.

And he had to make a profit to keep his father's legacy alive. No way would he let Sullivan Ranch go without a fight.

Rose appeared at the screen. "Come on inside. Too dark now to appreciate all Will's hard work. You can see the ranch tomorrow. It's supposed to be a beautiful day. Did you see that red sky?"

Will held the door open.

As she moved past, Annie raised a knowing brow at him. "Told you so," she whispered.

Will merely smiled.

"Wait until you see all the changes around here. Will's put this place on the map. Did he tell you about the web page?"

Annie grinned. "Yes, I heard."

Rose wiped her hands on her apron and stepped back as Annie hopped inside. "Oh, and, Will, that was for you, that gal from church who keeps pestering you." Rose frowned. "I've already forgotten her name. Well, no never mind. I let her know you're too busy to chitchat, and to call back tomorrow."

"What?" Annie taunted from inside the house. "Will has a girlfriend?"

Grabbing the suitcases, he strode past the kitchen. The aroma of fresh blackberry pie accompanied him down the hallway.

"I do not have a girlfriend," he called, depositing the bags on the rag rug in Annie's old room.

The fact was he rarely dated and took pains not encourage anyone in any way. Will had come to terms with the path he must take long ago. It could never include marriage.

"Why, our Will is considered quite a catch these days, don't you know?" Rose said, proud as any mother.

Annie released a strangled laugh at Rose's words and slapped her palm on the heavy oak table.

"What's so funny about that?" After drying his hands, Will balled up the dish towel and shot, hitting his target dead-on where she sat.

Pulling the cloth off her head, Annie flung the fabric back.

He neatly dodged.

"Okay, you two. No horseplay in the house," Rose reprimanded, picking up the towel from the floor. She opened the refrigerator and grabbed a large foil-covered plate.

"Yes, ma'am." Will's fingers snaked out to grab a slice of roast beef just as Rose uncovered the platter. He popped the tidbit into his mouth.

When he turned he found Annie inspecting

him. "What?" he asked, uncomfortable with her assessment.

"N-Nothing." She quickly glanced away.

"Come on. You're up to something."

Annie cleared her throat and turned back, her usual mischievous smile in place. "I wondered if I crossed my eyes and looked real hard I might be able to figure out what all the fuss is about."

"Huh?"

"All those women chasing you."

"Oh, knock it off," he growled. "Now, what do you want to drink?"

"Anything without caffeine, please," she said. A frown settled on her face. "Suddenly I'm not tired at all, and that is not good."

"Having insomnia, honey?" Rose asked. "You sleep on the plane at all?"

"The only place I've managed to get any decent sleep was in Will's truck."

"Is that the story of my life or what? I bore women to sleep."

"You should be honored. I don't nod off for just anyone, you know."

The circles beneath her eyes told Will she didn't exaggerate. He knew it wasn't only plane rides keeping her awake. What happened over there that continued to haunt her nights? She'd refused to discuss the accident on the phone.

"What else do you want out of here, Rose?" He motioned to the refrigerator.

"Grab that spicy mustard Annie likes, and the blackberry pie from the counter."

"Oh, well, now I know I'm in heaven. Blackberry pie." Annie licked her lips. She stood and awkwardly leaned against the chair back, then hopped to the cupboard.

"I'll get whatever you need," Will said.

She pulled out a plate. "I'm not helpless. Now please slide that pie over here."

"You can't eat dessert first." He held the tin barely out of her grasp.

"Watch me." Annie grabbed the pie from Will's hands. She set it down and transferred a generous chunk onto her plate then to her mouth. Slowly chewing and swallowing, she closed her eyes for a moment in silent appreciation. "Nobody cooks like Rose." A fork pointed at him, she continued, "You're spoiled rotten."

"Got that straight." He swiped a small crumb that had fallen from her fork to the polished wood table. Tasting the morsel, he stopped and relished the rightness of having the people he cared about most gathered together in his kitchen. Heartfelt words slipped out before he was aware of it. "It's so good to have you back."

Annie paused. "Thank you, Will." She sounded almost shy.

"Are you saying all I have to do to keep you here is keep the pie coming?" Rose asked.

"That'll do it," Annie agreed, eyes still locked on Will as she sat back down. "Of course, you'll be rolling me down the front steps when I leave," she added.

"You just got here. Don't start talking about leaving," Rose moaned.

"Rose," Will reminded softly. They'd discussed this topic after Annie's phone call.

Don't get your hopes up, he'd said.

He thought Rose would collapse when she heard about the attack on the Kenyan border clinic. A bullet hit Annie's leg. They'd received a late-night phone message from the U.S. Embassy informing them Annie was in a Nairobi hospital.

Will's jaw clenched as he remembered. Then and there he decided to call and demand she come home—at least until she healed. Before the call went through he'd already determined he wouldn't allow her to draw him into an argument.

Her quick wit and sharp tongue he could handle. The acquiescence he heard in her voice was a sucker punch to his gut. Annie was scared and wanted nothing more at that moment than to return to the States.

But for how long?

Now that she was here, it would be difficult for Rose to let her go again.

"I know, I know," Rose said, stirring the potato salad with vengeance. She turned her head, using the corner of her apron to wipe moisture from her eyes.

Rose's heartfelt response slammed into Will.

A surge of protectiveness for the woman who'd mothered him for so long welled in his chest.

He glanced at Annie, who sat at the table looking miserable and seeming unsure what to do. For the first time in a long time, Will sent up a prayer. He didn't set much stock in them anymore, but Annie defied rational thought. Will was more than frustrated, so he prayed for some kind of intervention, hoping there was a way to make Annie stay.

Chapter Two

Will sat in the rocking chair with one boot propped on the railing and the other on the porch.

Alone with the stars. The time of day he liked best. It was quiet enough to hear an occasional car out on the service road a mile away. The soft night breeze brought only a rustle from the trees and a whinny from the stable.

He used to come out here at night mad and frustrated, trying to make sense of life. Now, after years of tangling with his demons, he'd finally found an uncertain peace. He imagined his father sitting in the same beat-up rocker and coming to similar conclusions.

Seeing Annie again brought all the conflicting thoughts back. Vibrant and alive, she had a future that was hers to take.

For only brief seconds did he despair his own destiny. Then he pushed the negative thoughts away. He wouldn't allow them to control his life ever again.

He'd gone to the wall and back with God on this. Huntington's.

There was a fifty-fifty chance he had the disease that slowly destroyed his father.

A mere toss of the coin.

Those odds were what had kept him awake at night when he was younger. He'd been haunted day and night after his father's death. Every tremor, every stumbled step reminded Will of the deterioration that forced his father into a wheelchair and then to the bed that became his final prison.

Huntington's was the Sullivan family secret. Only Rose knew, and she'd honored Will's privacy.

The first time they'd discussed the subject she'd begged him to be tested.

He couldn't do that, even for Rose.

If he was negative, sure, the anxiety would be over. But if he was positive, he'd spend every moment of every day anticipating symptoms, seeing even more demons around every corner.

There was no medical advantage to being tested. A positive test result couldn't tell when he'd actually develop the disease or to what degree. It only meant he was positive for the gene. There would be even more unanswered questions. Another can of worms to deal with.

It was about the time Annie left he realized he had two choices: walk away from God or walk with Him. He'd chosen the latter, knowing there was no way he could make this journey alone.

Will planned to savor each day, appreciating what

was set before him. He had the ranch and his friends. Life was pretty darn good. Yes, his was an uncertain peace. But peace, nonetheless.

On his terms.

Just the way he liked things.

He stared out at the land. Even in the darkness he recognized every landmark on the property, from the maple trees in front of the house to the horse barn rising to the right, to the silhouette of the peach orchard far to the north.

Sullivan Ranch. His legacy.

But could he hold on to that legacy?

Will's ears perked at a sound from in the house. He stopped the easy motion of the chair and listened. The screen creaked and pushed open.

He tipped back his head to look.

Annie wore Rose's plaid flannel robe, twisted, with the collar tucked in. Her hair stood up around her head, like some sort of wayward angel.

"Who've you been wrestling?"

"That silly bed, of course. It has more lumps than I remembered."

"Hey, princess, Rose replaced that mattress as soon as she found out you were coming back."

"Really? Then I guess I have more lumps than I remembered." She rubbed her hip.

He chuckled and got to his feet. "Here, sit down." As she limped past he pulled out the collar of her robe. "You look like you stuck your finger in a light socket."

"Flatterer." With nimble fingers she smoothed

down her hair and pushed the strands away from her face. "What are you doing up, Will?"

"A lot on my mind."

"Me, too." Easing into the chair, she glanced at him, dark eyes sparkling with mischief. "I guess it's a bit early for breakfast."

"A bit." He glanced at the luminous dial of his watch, then gave her a wink. "But not too early for a midnight snack."

"Blackberry pie." They said the words together and laughed.

Will stood. "What do you want to drink?"

"Milk," she said, using her good leg to gently rock the chair. "And thanks so much, Will."

He returned moments later, their snacks on a tray, which he set on the rail of the porch. "You know, it's getting mighty annoying the way you thank me for every single thing."

"But." She swallowed hard and blinked furiously. "I mean, it's not like I live here anymore. I don't want to mess up your schedule and be a bother."

So that was what this was all about.

"Annie, we're your family. This is your home."

"No." She reached out a hand to touch his arm and he stepped back.

Annie cleared her throat. "I'm—I'm grateful you and Rose took me in. You certainly didn't need another mouth to feed, and I'm so appreciative that you put up with me all those years. But, Will, Sullivan Ranch is *your* home. Not mine."

"I don't want your gratitude." He paused and

stared at her. Understanding suddenly broke through the emotions crowding his mind. "Is that why you didn't come back after college?"

"I did come back."

"For less than a year."

She clasped and unclasped her hands.

"Why did you go to Kenya?" He wanted to understand. *Needed to understand.*

"I had to find my own life, my own place in this world. I honestly felt called to medical missions. Besides, I was itching to get out and see the world." She tightened the belt on the robe. "They needed me over there, and there wasn't a good reason not to stay."

"Even though the situation was tense?" He ran his fingers through his hair. The thought of Annie putting herself at risk chilled him through and through.

"It wasn't really. Not at first. When they attacked the clinic—" She hitched in a breath. "For the first time in my life I was faced with my own mortality. I realized I might never see the ranch again. The next thing I knew, the embassy was pulling us out. I wasn't sure where I would go." She met his gaze. "The timing. Your phone call."

"You wouldn't have called?" He turned away and stared out into the night, frozen for a moment by the shock delivered by the truth.

"I know none of this makes any sense to you, Will."

He shook his head and glanced down at her. "Sure

it does. Finally everything is making sense. And I could wring your neck."

"Good," she interrupted. "Then nothing's changed, because you're always wanting to wring my neck." She smiled sweetly.

He refused to give in to her humor. Instead, he demanded, "How could you question where you would go?"

She shrugged and bit her lip. "I'm sorry, but the longer I stayed away the harder it was to come back."

Crouching down, he took her hands in his. They were small and soft, the skin chilled. "Tell me what happened."

Taking a large breath, she stared ahead, her gaze a million miles away. "I can't. I wish I could but I seem to have blocked it out. Sometimes at night it starts to come back to me and then—" her gaze connected with his "—nothing. I don't think I'm ready to remember anything but what they've told me."

Will shook his head.

Annie's gaze shifted and she stared over his shoulder. "Look," she said. "The moon."

He glanced behind him. Sure enough, it was a full moon, unusually bright with a luminescent glow.

"And the way those stars are scattered across the sky," Annie said. "It's like diamonds on velvet."

"I don't think I could ever leave this place," he said, leaning against the rail.

"You don't have to," she whispered.

* * *

Annie scrunched the pillow over her face to block out the annoying sunlight streaming through the lace curtains. At some point in the night her body finally adjusted, and gave in to the luxury of a mattress over the familiar cot she'd been sleeping on for the past two years. She ushered a thank-you to God for the few hours of real rest she'd gotten last night.

A yelp of pain escaped when she sat up. Her leg was painfully stiff from being in the same position so long. The stitches pulled against her skin. She ran a hand over the area. Thankfully, it remained cool to her touch, with no signs of infection peeking out from the gauze. Today she'd remove the dressing and let the incision air.

Annie glanced around. Her room. Except for dusting, everything had remained untouched. When the breeze from the open window whispered past, she could smell the familiar fragrance of lavender mingled with furniture polish. Rose had tucked handmade lavender sachets into every drawer.

The bedroom truly was the only substantial thing Annie had ever called her own. Of course it wasn't really hers. But a young girl could pretend it was her very own room and pretend she had a real family.

The small space had been a nondescript guest room when Annie had arrived. Over the next year or two Rose had very quietly transformed everything, enjoying every minute of painting the walls, sewing the curtains and picking out colors for a quilt.

Annie fingered the soft, gently worn fabric of the hand-pieced and machine-sewn quilt. "Around The World," Rose called the pattern. Colors of peach and cream blended together into a soothing patchwork design, with a pale green border.

Around the world. Well, she had certainly done that. All her life, it seemed. She had traveled from town to town with her gypsy mother until being brought to the ranch to stay with Rose.

Why Rose? She'd often asked the question during those first years, trying to make sense of everything.

"Your mother and I were neighbors when we were children. We grew up together. She spent a lot of time at my house," Rose explained.

"But what about my grandparents?" Annie asked.

"Leanne always told me her papa was in the navy and her momma was restless."

"Restless." Annie said the words aloud to the empty room. Was that her legacy? Restless.

As promised, Leanne returned six months later, once she and her husband were settled. When her new stepfather began to take notice of Annie, Leanne was quick to return her daughter to the ranch with the necessary papers for Rose to share guardianship.

Annie wondered if Rose had heard from her mother recently. While Leanne sent the occasional birthday card, the last real contact had been a quick, unexpected phone call when Annie turned seventeen, to let her know her mother was again divorced. At the time Annie feared Leanne would come and take her away. But no, she was headed to California to follow a "get rich quick" scheme.

Wiggling her toes and stretching her arms, Annie reached for the flannel robe she'd tossed on the end of the four-poster bed. Frustrating as it was, she would have to use the cane until her leg limbered up.

Her stomach growled, and she was both surprised and thankful. It seemed her appetite was back with a vengeance. Coffee and more pie sounded like a wonderful way to start the day. With any luck, Will hadn't already finished off both.

She fished in her tapestry bags for her hairbrush then headed for the private bathroom, throwing water on her face and brushing her teeth, before grabbing the cane. Voices reached her as she hobbled carefully down the oak floor of the hallway.

Annie paused in the kitchen entry and discovered there was a guest at the table. Will sat across from a sophisticated blonde in a cream linen suit who gestured in conversation.

She inched back out of the room.

"About time you got up. We were debating whether or not to wake you for dinner," Will called. A hint of a smile played on his strong mouth.

"Dinner? What are you talking about?" She glanced at the black, wrought-iron rooster clock on the wall. Three o'clock? "I slept over twelve hours."

"You needed that sleep," he said.

"Apparently," Annie admitted. "I missed church."

"Are you kidding me?" Will laughed.

Rose pulled out a chair. "Come sit down, honey."

"Oh, no, no." Annie shook her head. "You have a guest. I don't want to interrupt. Besides, I'm not dressed."

"Don't be silly. This is just Mrs. Reilly," Rose said, dismissing Annie's concerns with a wave of her hand. "Now sit yourself down." She pulled out a chair. "I've got a fresh pot of coffee brewing."

The woman seated at the table raised a perfectly arched brow at Rose's remark.

"That sounds wonderful," Annie admitted. She carefully lowered herself into a ladder-backed chair.

"Annie, this is Margaret Reilly," Will said. "She and her husband, Ed, are involved in a joint venture with Sullivan Ranch."

Annie offered the woman her hand. The blonde's grip was strong and businesslike as her assessing gaze met Annie's head-on. A second glance at the woman's polished features and Annie realized Margaret was her own mother's age.

"Call me Margaret. I'm delighted to finally meet Will's little sister."

Little sister? Her glance darted to Will, who had suddenly become preoccupied with the floor tile.

Well, why was she surprised? The words only verified what she knew all along.

"I understand you're a nurse," Margaret said. "I

don't know how you do it. That sort of work definitely has to be a calling."

"Annie *is* called. Did you know she had a full-ride academic scholarship to the University of Tulsa?" Rose spoke with pride. As she talked, she filled a mug with steaming coffee and set it on the table in front of Annie.

"TU? I'm impressed. So, what are your plans now that you're back? How long are you visiting?"

"Visiting?" Rose interrupted, her voice taking on an edge. "Why, Annie is family."

Margaret gave a small, tight smile. "So you'll probably be looking for a job, and I know they're desperate for nurses in Oklahoma City. I have a colleague who is on the board of several hospitals. I'd be happy to give her your name."

"OK City is too far," Rose said. "They're hiring right here in T-town."

"I'm not really sure what I'll do once the doctor releases me," Annie answered. "But thank you for thinking of me."

"Oh, yes. Will mentioned your accident. You were overseas."

"But she's not going back. Right, Annie?" Rose asked with concern.

Annie reached out to put her hand over Rose's. The conversation was spiraling out of control.

Will cleared his throat.

Annie recognized the pained expression on his face as a desperate plea to change the subject.

"Have we got any fruit in the house?" he asked, with a quick glance around.

"Fruit?" Rose asked, distracted. "What on earth are you talking about? There's fruit in the basket, where it always is." She grabbed the willow basket off the counter and dropped it squarely in front of Will.

Margaret stood. "I must get back to the house. We're hosting that big charity buffet tonight." She paused to give Will her complete attention. "I can still count on you to be there, right?"

Will frowned slightly, confusion evident his face. "Tonight?" He scratched his head. "Did I know about this?"

Margaret gathered her leather clutch. "You certainly did. Ed and I both told you there will be several very important contacts for the ranch attending this party, including several well-connected young ladies that you certainly must meet."

Margaret Reilly was pointed in her plan for matchmaking. No doubt she'd find the perfect wife.

The perfect wife for Will Sullivan.

The sharp pain of realization made Annie wince. She blinked and mindlessly lifted the coffee mug to her lips, taking a swig of the hot beverage. The immediate result burned her mouth and brought tears to her eyes. With a noise of pain she swallowed.

"You okay?" Will asked, jumping to his feet.

"Hot. Hot," Annie sputtered.

He moved quickly to the sink, filling a glass with tap water. "Here, drink."

She did, swishing the cool and soothing water over the inside of her scalded mouth before swallowing.

"Goodness, child. Are you all right?" Rose questioned.

Humiliated, Annie nodded. *Oh, this day was starting out fine. Little sister and child, all in one brief fiasco.*

"It was nice to meet you, Margaret," Annie said, hoping to move past the awkward incident.

"My pleasure, Annie. I know we'll see each other often. My husband, Ed, and I work very closely with Sullivan Ranch." She turned to Will. "Don't we, Will?"

Will gave a short nod.

"I'm sorry. What is it you do?" Annie asked.

Margaret gave a bemused smile. "Why, Ed is the CEO of KidCare."

Annie raised a brow.

"Oh, my. You have been gone for a while."

"KidCare is an international children's ministry consulting firm based in Tulsa," Will answered.

"Basically we connect and support children's charities, ministries and youth organizations," Margaret said.

"How does that involve Will?" Annie asked.

"Ed had several great ideas and came to me with a business plan about eighteen months ago," Will explained. "Sullivan Ranch will be hosting events for KidCare. In return, KidCare backs the operations and promote the events."

Annie nodded. She imagined the publicity alone

was a boost for the ranch. "That sounds really exciting."

"Oh, it is," Margaret assured her. "Sullivan Ranch has their first big program coming up. A local denomination is holding a get-together for their junior high kids from across the Tulsa area. They'll be camping out right here."

"Where, here?" Annie asked.

"Right here on the ranch," Will said. "I'll show you around later. You won't believe the changes. I've added a few cabins on the other side of the peach trees, near the Dearborne property line. There's a campground, too." His eyes lit up and his face, normally a mask of composure, seemed almost animated.

"Really?" Annie said. "What a terrific idea. I can't wait for a tour."

Margaret wrinkled her nose. "I'll pass on the camping, but I will be coordinating the catering for the barbecue."

Rose coughed. "I keep telling you I can handle a little barbecue," she said, while giving the already sparkling countertops a brisk rubdown with her sponge.

"I'm certain you can, Rose," Margaret returned. "But there will be about fifty or so campers, and I wouldn't think of imposing upon your goodwill. Besides, there are health regulations we must adhere to."

Rose inhaled sharply.

Ouch. Business or not, Margaret didn't understand

who ruled the culinary roost at Sullivan Ranch. Rose O'Shea did, and she'd done it single-handedly for over twenty years.

"What time is that party tonight?" Will asked, interrupting the uneasy silence.

"Seven. Of course you'll be there early so we can take care of some KidCare business before everyone arrives," Margaret said. She caught Will's eye, making it very clear she expected full cooperation.

"Probably won't make the party early," Will finally answered Margaret, as he walked to the sink and rinsed his mug. "This is Annie's first full day back."

Margaret blinked with surprise. "I see. Then we'll expect you at seven. Don't forget a tie."

"No, ma'am, I won't."

There was a strained silence before Margaret spoke again. "Ed has those brochures ready for you. They're in the car if you'd like to collect the box now."

Will pursed his lips, then nodded and grabbed his hat.

Margaret adjusted her jacket. When she turned to Annie, control was back in place. "I'll see you again, Annie. We'll plan to do lunch once you're settled."

Annie smiled, though somehow she just couldn't see her and Margaret doing lunch.

"Thank you for the coffee, Rose," Margaret added, following Will.

Rose gave a curt nod.

When they were well out of earshot, Annie rubbed her hands together. "Well, that was fun."

"Don't even get me started," Rose fumed, clearing the table. "That woman thinks she can run Will, the same as she runs her husband." Rose took a deep breath. "Now, what do you want to eat?"

Annie opened her mouth to suggest pie, but shut it quickly as Rose continued: "And don't you dare say pie."

Chapter Three

❧

The old ranch Jeep, a rusty black model minus doors, roared to life. Will shifted gears, guiding the vehicle along the bumpy dirt and gravel road, leaving a wake of dust.

"Sure you're up to this?" Will asked.

Annie pushed her windswept hair out of her eyes and tucked the strands behind her ears. She slapped a navy ball cap emblazoned with the University of Tulsa logo on her head, and turned in the seat to face him. "Are you kidding? After all that sleep?"

"But your leg?"

She had pushed the seat back as far as possible to accommodate and protect her extended left leg. Will glanced down at the uncovered wound. Her pant leg was rolled up to her knee, and with the dressing off he could see the incision on the back of her calf. It ran horizontal, at least four inches, with a small vertical zigzag. Tight stitches pulled the skin together. Several large abrasions around the area were scabbed and healing.

The bullet, Annie had told him on the phone, penetrated the muscle and then exited, leaving the area a nasty mess. The surgeon opened the area to clean and remove shards of glass along with embedded dirt and gravel from her fall. Now that the infection was under control, the wound appeared to be healing nicely.

So why was it he cringed every time he glanced at her leg? Will did not consider himself fainthearted. He could handle any number of emergencies related to the animals on the ranch, yet he found himself skittish about this. Maybe because it was Annie who'd been hurt. An involuntary shudder went clear through him.

"You've seen worse accidents at the rodeo."

"Not the same thing. Trust me."

"Well, you're going to have to deal with it. I hurt my leg. It's healing. End of story."

He said nothing to her curt response, noting only that she seemed out of sorts since Margaret Reilly's visit.

In fact Rose was the same way. Plain cranky.

Rose he understood. She'd run the Sullivan house since his mother left. At times he wondered what kept Rose here in Granby with him and the ranch. She had never married, often saying the Sullivans were all the family she needed, and later including Annie in her circle of love.

His father had often told him a kitchen was only big enough for one woman. Will figured Annie didn't count because she was like a daughter to Rose.

Margaret Reilly? Well, that was another story. She got on Rose's last nerve.

On several occasions during strategic planning meetings at the ranch, Will had to pull Margaret aside to explain Rose's role at the ranch wasn't simply housekeeper. No, Rose O'Shea couldn't be defined by the words *housekeeper* or *cook*. Margaret had a hard time understanding, but at least she'd stopped giving out suggestions for redecorating the house and reorganizing the kitchen in front of the feisty older woman.

He wasn't too sure why Margaret irritated Annie. Must be a woman thing.

The campground appeared in the distance and Will pointed as they approached. The perfect spot, it was nestled in a protective shelter of trees. The tall redbuds, elms and birches were planted by his grandfather William Sullivan.

"Finished those cabins a few weeks ago," he told Annie. "Along with the shower facility. The covered areas over there are for picnics, barbecues and activities."

Six cabins, each able to accommodate four campers, stood in a semicircle to the right. The clearing to the left was for pitching tents.

"You've got showers and toilets?"

"Don't want them coming to the house, do I?"

"This is roughing it, Okie style? Those cabins are adorable."

"Adorable?" Will nearly choked on the word. "They're not adorable."

"Sure they are. So you're planning on quite a few campouts?"

"More than quite a few. We're booked nearly every weekend from now to the end of the summer."

Annie's eyes widened. "Will, that's a lot of work."

"You bet it is, and this has been over a year in the making. Besides campouts we've got one-night events like hayrides and church meetings. The riding lessons have picked up too."

"Who does the lessons?"

"I wish I could say I do them all, but mostly I rely on Chris LaFarge and his wife, Joanie. Chris is a vet tech over at Doc Jones's practice."

"You're busy."

"There's an understatement. I spend most of my time on the phone troubleshooting and scheduling. The frustrating part is trying to get any real work done in between calls. Getting to be a joke."

"Sounds like you need a personal assistant."

"Margaret said the same thing."

"That's because she probably has a personal assistant."

"Yeah, well, I can't afford that kind of expense. By the spring I'll know if I can draw my own paycheck as an employee. There's no way I can bring anyone else on board at this point."

"So explain to me again how the Reillys play into all this?"

"Ed Reilly came to me with the idea. KidCare is the middleman in this operation. They negotiate the programs and outsource to operations like Sullivan Ranch. KidCare takes a percentage of profits right off the top along with a fee I pay them for things like marketing. I deal mostly with Margaret on a day-to-day basis."

Annie tilted her head, listening.

"You've never heard of KidCare, but trust me, for a homegrown operation, they're huge. Lots of influence and lots of money. At first Ed offered to finance the changes I'd need," Will continued. "But that didn't sit well with me. I'm fortunate KidCare is interested in working with Sullivan Ranch, but I don't want them to own me." He adjusted the rim of his straw Stetson.

"How *did* you pay for the work?" Clearly Annie wasn't shy about asking questions.

"I sold the land in the north pasture to the Dearbornes." Will shifted uncomfortably. *Just saying the words made him nervous.*

"That's almost…" Annie blinked hard. "That's almost a third of the ranch."

"I know. I know. To tell you the truth, it scared me spitless. Fact is, the past few years I've been barely squeaking by with the horse boarding and my inheritance. Ed came along when I was seriously contemplating the need to sell everything."

She sucked in a breath. "Sell Sullivan Ranch?"

Will seconded her reaction. He gazed out through the mud-spattered windshield, his vision taking in the pecan grove and the small peach and apple orchard. "It's been a long time since this place has been a working ranch." He pointed to the pasture beyond the trees. "There haven't been cattle out there since before my dad got sick, and that was a long time ago."

Quiet filled the Jeep as Will paused, his hand moving the clutch back and forth in and out of neutral. "This ranch is all I know. But something had to give, and I just couldn't see the past as a way to the future."

He turned to Annie, the knot in his stomach tightening. "Am I wrong?"

"No, Will. I think you're right. Besides, the entire project has changed you. It's good to see you so enthusiastic. I'm really happy for you. But how are you going to do it all by yourself?"

"Slowly. Very slowly. I started with a plan, and so far things have worked. At first I focused on getting the ranch in shape, starting with routine maintenance. Then I contracted to have the work done for the new campgrounds. There were inspections and zoning red tape until I couldn't see straight."

Annie gave a thoughtful nod as he spoke.

"Now I have a couple reliable college kids on the weekend. They'll help set things up and do the tear down. Chris and Joanie get the horses fed and exercised in the evening. Gives me a break."

"Still leaves a lot for you to do. Maintenance of the ranch and bookkeeping, and now these Kid-Care projects are rolling. What are you going to do when you start getting outside reservations, besides KidCare?"

Will grinned and his pleasure soared. *She got it. Annie understood.*

"Already started getting outside reservations. That's why I'm booked almost solid." He grinned, unable to contain his pride. "Hey, it's hard work. Any new venture is. They say you can expect to work twenty-four-seven for the first few years to launch a new business. I'm prepared to do that."

And he was. There wasn't any extra time left over to brood on the past or worry about the future. No time to think about Huntington's these days.

"I'm surprised you know if you're coming or going."

Will laughed. She wasn't far off the mark. "Annie, the place seems to be exploding with ideas. I'd like to expand and put in Quonset huts and a full kitchen and hold full camps Monday through Friday, all summer long. The place would be a Christian dude ranch. I know it's not a new idea. There are plenty around the area. But it's still a pretty lucrative opportunity, considering we're smack-dab in the middle of the Bible Belt."

"That's a terrific vision. I can see it happening."

Excitement sizzled through him as he spoke. "Can you, Annie? Because I really can." He fiddled with a thread on his jeans. "Sometimes I'm so fired up I could burst with needing to talk."

"Will Sullivan a chatterbox. Now that's a new one."

Will paused for a moment, taking in the picture Annie made. A smile teased her lips, and her eyes brimmed with laughter. Unable to resist, he reached out and gently adjusted the crooked ball cap on her head.

"Better?" she asked quietly.

"Perfect," Will returned.

They sat in silence for a few minutes, and Will knew that at this moment he was more content than he had been in a very long time.

"Now I remember why they call it Green Country," she said, her gaze taking in the thick, lush grass and the leafy trees around them.

"Pretty, huh?"

"Yes, but I just realized I missed the azaleas blooming."

"Stick around. They bloom every year."

She frowned.

"You missed most of tornado season, too."

"That I don't miss," she said. "Remember that year one hit the barn and took your cow two miles down the road?"

"Yeah. Amazing old Daisy was unhurt. Mad as all get-out, but not a thing wrong with that cow."

"Rose was worried sick. How is old Daisy?"

"I don't even know. But she hasn't changed a bit. Still stubborn and contrary, but Rose flat out refuses to let me sell that cow. Says my dad loved old Daisy and she's part of my heritage."

"Kindred spirits," Annie said, laughing.

"You mean Rose and Dad, or Daisy and Rose?"

"I don't think I should answer that."

Will took a deep breath of Oklahoma air and

pushed the wind from his lungs. "End of May is about the best time of year, don't you think?"

Annie nodded.

"We'll be complaining about the heat and humidity soon enough, but now…warm days. Cool nights. This has been an especially kind spring, too. The grass will stay green well into summer after all the rain we've had."

"I don't think I'm even going to notice the humidity here after living in Kenya."

He'd driven the Jeep in a large circle around the ranch and as they pulled close to the rear of the house, Annie waved for him to stop.

"Oh, my goodness. What happened to Rose's garden?"

"We moved the garden over by the pond. There's a gazebo there now, too."

"Then what's that?" She pointed to a large area surrounded by a white picket fence. Inside, the dark red clay had obviously been tilled and fertilized. Neat rows of small plants were staked as far as her eye could see.

"Pumpkin patch."

"The world's largest pumpkin patch?"

"Pretty much. Can't you see it in the fall, with kids all over the place picking out pumpkins?"

"Yes. I can." She scrutinized the area, then spoke again. "What about pony rides and a small animal-petting zoo? You know, calves and lambs. A donkey. You could probably get the animal shelter to bring out puppies and kittens for adoption. Make it a yearly event."

"Now why didn't I think of that?"

As she waved a hand to gesture with increased enthusiasm, Will could almost see the ideas percolating under that ball cap on her head.

"Add bales of hay and a few scarecrows to give it a real harvest theme. Why, I bet you could sell Sullivan peaches and pecans and Rose's pies, too."

Will snapped his fingers. "You're a genius, Annie."

"I have my moments."

"Let me know if you have any more."

Annie laughed at his words.

He glanced over at the stable. "I haven't even shown you the horses yet, have I?"

She hesitated. "No. But have you checked the time? You've got that fundraiser at seven."

Disappointment slid over him as he confirmed her words with a quick look at his watch. He'd much rather be riding around the ranch with Annie than playing nice at the Reillys' party.

Will stuck a finger into the collar of his dress shirt, searching for breathing room. Giving up, he unbuttoned the top button and loosened the noose. *Why was he here?* Then he remembered. Networking.

He sipped a tall, chilled glass of sweet tea and watched Margaret Reilly flit around the great room of the Reilly home. A butterfly in a pink suit, she checked on each and every one of her guests. Detailed instructions were given to the caterers before she floated across the pristine white carpet to light next to him.

"You aren't eating?" she said.

"Not real hungry," Will admitted, eyeing the buffet table.

Long tables were covered with pink linens and centerpieces of fresh spring flowers, all coordinating perfectly with the hostess's ensemble. Serving platters were laden with delicacies Will hadn't attempted to identify. Fact was he wasn't much into fancy food. A plain meat-and-potatoes kind of guy, he preferred a good steak every time.

He knew he was out of his league here among the Tulsa religious elite gathered for the fundraiser. A simple rancher, he was trying to become a savvy businessman, but small talk was not his forte.

If he had his way he'd never leave the ranch. Will had majored in business, while commuting between Granby and home, but he couldn't grab his degree and get back to the ranch fast enough. He had no aspirations of grandeur beyond keeping Sullivan Ranch afloat and contributing to a community that supported him through the tough times.

He loved the land, liked hard work and enjoyed getting dirty.

Dressing up made him uncomfortable, and today he'd put on a suit and tie and Sunday shoes—twice. His feet longed for the comfort of his worn Justins.

Gaze drifting, he observed the uniformed staff

through the French doors. The Reillys sure could throw a party. Things would move outside anytime now. The buffet dinner and social time were to be followed by a silent auction on the grounds.

Waiters made last-minute preparations for seating along the huge patio area, near the heated pool where sparkly frosted lights hung between huge maple trees. An impromptu stage covered by a white canvas tent had been erected on the lawn. A small ensemble played classical melodies in the background. At the end of the patio another long serving table boasted lavish dessert trays and silver coffee urns.

"I can ask Chef to prepare something for you," Margaret offered.

"I'm sorry?" Will said, realizing he'd been miles away.

"I said I'd be happy to ask Chef to prepare something for you."

He gave a small laugh. Was he that transparent? He felt certain he stuck out as a real greenhorn in this crowd and said so.

"Not at all," Margaret said. "Actually, you and Ed are a lot alike."

A red warning flag went up. Margaret was preparing to launch into one of her Ed stories.

"Would you excuse me a minute, Margaret?" He was long overdue for a dose of fresh air.

He moved slowly, stopping to greet a business acquaintance, and then paused to examine the original Western artwork scattered throughout the room.

Grabbing a fresh tea, he slipped out the side patio doors when Margaret wasn't looking.

The night air remained warm with barely a breeze. A hand in his pocket, Will stood for minutes watching the few clouds in the clear, dark sky move across a blanket of stars.

"Beautiful night."

Will didn't have to turn to realize Ed Reilly had joined him. "It is. Wouldn't trade Oklahoma for any other place on the planet."

"Me either," Ed agreed. "But you ought to be inside meeting those young ladies Margaret has lined up for you. They come from important Tulsa families."

Will turned to face the older man. Tall and blond with silver shot through the temples, he had one obvious thing in common with his wife. Ed Reilly was accustomed to getting what he wanted.

"Sounds like she's negotiating a business deal," Will observed.

"Take some advice from a fellow who has been around the block, Will. A good partnership can lay a solid foundation for a long-term relationship. Don't rule it out."

"I'll give that some thought, sir."

While he said the appropriate words, Will knew he wasn't interested in Ed's definition of a long-term business arrangement. Fact of the matter was he believed in love. Hadn't seen much of it, but somewhere in the back of his heart he knew that if the Huntington's wasn't a block in his road of life and he was in the position to consider marriage, he wouldn't consider it for anything less than love. A forever and ever, all-encompassing love.

"Nice party," Will said.

Ed chuckled, knowing he'd been sidestepped. "That it is. A fine party, indeed. Hope the good food and fellowship encourages folks to dig deep into their wallets. We're supporting a very worthy cause tonight."

"I'm sure they will. Tulsa is a generous town."

"You're right, Will. Tulsa *is* a generous town. There is always someone willing to lend a helping hand."

"Yes, sir."

"My wife tells me everything is moving along well for the youth retreat."

Will nodded.

"I'll be out of town next week, but I know you two can handle things."

"I appreciate your confidence in me."

"You're doing a great job. Give it a year, eighteen months, and you'll start to reap the fruit of this venture."

"I hope so. Don't mind telling you I've spent more than a few sleepless nights."

"Success is not without risks. But you're motivated, a hard worker and a Godly man. Rare combination these days. Before you know it Sullivan Ranch will be bigger than you dreamed."

"From your lips to God's ears," Will said.

Ed chuckled.

Both men turned as the patio doors burst open and Margaret stood silhouetted against the lights of the party inside.

"Are you two hiding?" Margaret asked.

"Not at all, darling," Ed said. "Just mixing a little business with pleasure."

She nodded, unconvinced. "Will has a phone call. You can take it in Ed's study."

Margaret led Will across the carpet and down the hall. Her heels clicked a sharp staccato pattern on the imported Mexican tile as she led the way to the study, opening the massive oak doors. "I do hope you'll hurry," she said, as she left him alone in the room. "The party isn't over yet."

He reached for the receiver on the desk. "Sullivan here."

"Will, I'm so sorry to bother you." Annie's voice overflowed with emotion. "I tried your cell first."

Will fumbled in his pants pocket for his cell. He must have left it in the truck. "What's wrong?" he asked, prepared for the worst.

"Rose. She fell. I'm certain she broke her hip. The ambulance is taking her to St. Francis Hospital."

Chapter Four

Annie fidgeted in the uncomfortable waiting-room chair. She'd watched the frantic activity in the busy E.R. for the past thirty minutes, wishing she could step in and help.

Her stateside hospital experience had been a med-surg unit after graduation, right before she left for the medical mission position. Boring compared to what she'd observed here. The staff certainly had a formidable challenge. The traffic in and out of the automatic doors seemed heavier than the large medical clinic outside Dadaab. If anything, being on the outside looking in made her anxious to return to nursing.

When Will came through the glass doors she grabbed her cane and stood.

In a suit and tie he took her breath away. Her heart sped up and she had to will herself, as always, to act normal. She knew she was fooling herself if she thought she'd ever be blasé where Will was concerned.

Apparently she wasn't the only one. Several nurses looked up and continued staring, their admiring gazes following the tall handsome rancher as he moved with purpose through the lobby. A worried frown on his face, he inspected the room. His glance connected with Annie and in several quick strides he was at her side.

"How'd you get here so fast?" he asked. His concerned eyes were more charcoal than blue, reflecting the dark gray suit he wore.

"I drove the Jeep."

"*The Jeep?* That piece of junk is held together with two rubber bands and a piece of duct tape."

She laughed. "It did fine."

"How's your leg?" He stepped back and urged her to sit. "And I'd appreciate it if you didn't read me the riot act for asking."

"Who, me?" She slid into the chair, resting the cane across her legs.

"Uh-huh."

"Sorry if I was irritable. The leg really is okay."

Will nodded. "What's happening with Rose?"

"X-ray. I got an update from one of the nurses. She thinks they're going to admit her soon."

"Surgery?"

"I imagine so, but I haven't heard anything definite yet."

"She hurting?"

"Not anymore. They gave her a nice shot." Annie smiled slightly. "Rose was reciting her apple pie recipe in her sleep by the time they came with the gurney to take her for a CAT scan and then to X-ray. The staff was standing around taking notes."

"You're kidding."

"A little. You need to relax, Will."

"I wish I could." He shook his head. "We need to call her sister. I don't know if Rose told you Ellen moved back to Catoosa last year."

"I already called. Ellen is in the billing office now, filling out paperwork." Annie leaned over and pulled Will's cell phone from her hobo bag and handed it to him. "I borrowed this. You left it on the kitchen table. I hope that was okay?"

"Of course."

"Ellen happened to be in town and made it here about the same time I did."

Will's eyebrows rose. "Good deal." He yanked the striped tie off his neck and shoved the fabric into his suit coat pocket. "Tell me what happened again."

"Rose swears it was that barn cat. She'd gone outside to put scraps on the compost pile and the cat was trying to catch birds. She shooed him off, turned too fast, tripped and fell."

"That's all? How could she break a hip like that?"

"It happens. She got herself up and back in the house, but she called me because she was in pain. When I checked, one leg appeared a bit longer than the other and the hip hurt to touch. She couldn't bear weight, so I called an ambulance." Annie paused. "You know how she always complained about her hip when the weather changed. Maybe she has some arthritis or osteoporosis? I don't know, but broken hips are always a risk for someone her age."

"Her age? How old do you suppose Rose is?"

"I'm not sure. You know the rules. Weight and age are taboo. I'm guessing she's sixty-something. What do you think?"

"You're probably right. She and my dad were about the same age, and he would have been sixty-three."

Annie did the math in her head. His father was thirty-four when Will was born. That would have made him fifty-two when he died. So young.

Will sat down in the chair next to her, shoulders slumped.

"Are you okay?" Annie asked him.

"Me? Yeah, I'm fine. I just realized Rose has never had a sick day since I've known her." He ran a hand through his hair. "She's the rock in my life."

"I know. Me, too. I feel horrible thinking how I take her for granted."

Will took a deep breath and nodded.

A female staff member in navy scrubs and a white lab coat approached them. A black stethoscope hung around her neck along with a photo ID on a chain. She was somewhere in her midforties with dark blond hair pulled back into a ponytail.

"Are you Ms. O'Shea's family?"

"Yes," Will answered, helping Annie to her feet as he stood.

Annie gave a small smile at how he didn't hesitate when asked the question.

Family. Interesting thing about family. The three of them were closer than any family she knew. But it wasn't a blood connection. Rose had been Will's "mother" since he was eight. He hadn't heard from his biological mother since she left. How could that happen? How could a woman leave her child and husband? At least Leanne in her own way had left Annie to protect her. That counted for something, didn't it?

"Susan Wyatt," the woman said, introducing herself. She transferred the chart she held to her left hand to greet them both, shaking first Will's hand, then Annie's.

"I'm Will Sullivan. This is Annie Harris."

"Nice to meet you. I'm one of the staff orthopedic surgeons. I happened to be in-house checking on a patient, so the E.R. doctor asked me to see Ms. O'Shea."

Will nodded.

"I just reviewed the X-rays. It appears to be a reasonably clean fracture. Since she's resting comfortably we're going to schedule surgery for early tomorrow afternoon. We'll complete her workup, get an anesthesiology evaluation, then have her seen by the respiratory therapist and the physical therapy department. Generally we like to prepare our patients for what they can expect after surgery." She perused the chart, then looked up at them. "Any questions?"

"Can I stay in the room with her?" Annie asked.

"Probably. Unless we run into a problem, she'll

come right back to the orthopedic unit afterward. I don't know if you're aware, but there is a surgery family waiting room. They allow two family members to wait there during the surgery. It's on the first floor near the main lobby."

As they spoke with the doctor, Rose's sister joined them.

Ellen McAllister looked like Rose's spitting image, except she had brown hair styled short instead of Rose's trademark iron-gray topknot. Easily sisters, they shared similar features, including ample waists and bosoms.

Ellen reached for Annie's hand as she joined them.

"Dr. Wyatt, this is Rose's sister, Mrs. McAllister," Will said.

"I overheard your comments on the surgery," Ellen said. "Is this a hip socket replacement or what?"

"No," Dr. Wyatt assured her. "I just reviewed her films with the radiologist. The break wasn't bad. She'll have a simple pinning that involves an incision and literally pinning the femur together, then I'll sew her back up. She'll have a drain for a few days, and a catheter for the first twenty-four hours. They'll have her up and walking with a walker by the second day post-op."

"Wow. That fast," Will said on a breath. "When will she come home?"

"Most patients stay in the hospital five to seven days, depending on their health status before surgery and barring complications."

"How long until she's back to normal?" Ellen asked.

"That depends on the patient. But if everything goes as smooth as we think it will, I'd say three to six months, and you won't even remember she had the surgery. She's in good health and we haven't found any problems so far."

"That's amazing," Ellen said.

"It is, isn't it?" Dr. Wyatt agreed with a smile. "Are there any more questions?"

"What do you think caused the break?" Annie asked. "Any chance of osteoporosis?"

"The CAT scan will tell us more, but I don't suspect an unusual amount of deterioration. I'll have her on calcium after surgery to improve her bone density and send her home with a prescription. Hopefully it will prevent any problems in the future."

Ellen nodded. "Thank you for taking care of my sister," she added.

"My pleasure. You'll have to check with the admissions office to see what her room number is. You might want to get a cup of coffee or a bite to eat and give the staff a little time to get her settled in." She glanced at her watch. "It's later than I thought. The food court is probably closed, but the coffee shop is open. There are signs at the end of the corridor." As she spoke she pointed.

"Thanks again," Will said.

As the surgeon turned to depart she said, "I don't have any cards on me, but if you think of any more questions you can have the hospital switchboard page me."

It took Ellen two seconds to wrap her arms around Annie for a tight hug. "I have missed you, young lady."

Then she turned to Will.

"And don't you look handsome," she said with a cluck of her tongue. "You know those nurses have been eyeing you for the past ten minutes at least."

Will released an embarrassed chuckle and changed the subject. "Shall we hit the coffee shop?"

"More like the ladies' room," Annie said.

"So how are you, Will? Enjoying having Annie back?" Ellen asked, once Annie was out of earshot.

"You bet. I haven't had anyone to spar with except Rose for so long, it took me half the day to get back in form."

Ellen laughed. She lowered her voice and glanced around. "Don't tell on me, but I snuck into the X-ray area and saw my sister."

"Why am I not surprised?" Will shook his head.

"She was wailing that she'd gotten herself into a mess on Annie's first day back."

"That's ridiculous. This sure isn't her fault."

"I reminded her Annie isn't going to be leaving for any mission trips while Rose is on the mend. That improved her disposition considerably."

"Ellen," Will scolded.

"Oh, Annie will see right through that. She's a nurse, remember?"

Still, Will could easily imagine Rose becoming a drama queen if she thought it would postpone Annie's departure.

"By the way, I'll be staying at the ranch until my sister gets home."

"Why?" Will didn't mean the word to sound blunt, but he was surprised. Surely Ellen and Rose weren't of the opinion he couldn't fend for himself?

"Respectability, Will. You can't be staying alone at the house with a beautiful young woman and no chaperone."

"Beautiful young woman?"

"Annie."

Annie?

He'd thought of her as his buddy for so long. Not quite a sister, but not quite *not* a sister, either. Beautiful young woman? He shook his head. How had that snuck up on him?

"Sure. Sure. Okay. Thank you, Ellen."

"You're welcome. The pastor's wife and I are going to take turns staying at the hospital. We'll get help from the church ladies. I don't get up to Tulsa as much as I used to. Good opportunity for us to get caught up on our chitchat and our crocheting at the same time."

Will smiled, knowing she wasn't kidding.

"Annie will stay at the hospital tonight while I get my things out to the ranch."

"Okay," he answered. Not that he was going to argue with Ellen as she issued orders. She was so much like Rose he found it a little unnerving.

"I've written up a list of things that need to be done around the house," Rose said from her hospital bed.

"A list? That isn't a list. It's a novel. You wrote a book," Ellen said, as she combed her sister's hair and inserted bobby pins into the topknot.

From across the room, Will stared out the hospital window at the Tulsa night sky. With Ellen's comment he turned back. When his glance connected with Annie's, she cleared her throat to suppress a laugh.

"Will, you help Ellen and don't be letting Annie do the chores. She's still on the mend."

Annie opened her mouth to protest, but Rose kept talking, wagging a finger at Will, who moved to stand at the foot of her bed with his hat in his hands.

"Do not let Margaret Reilly near my kitchen," she huffed. "And I saw her eyeing the furniture in the family room on Sunday. If I come home and find she's rearranged the house, why I'll…"

"Calm down," Will said. "Where did you get that idea? Margaret isn't interested in redecorating the house."

"Ha. That woman hasn't learned where her business ends and mine starts."

"Rose."

"Rose O'Shea," Ellen scolded.

"I'm just saying."

Will approached the head of the bed. Resting his hands on the metal rail, he leaned over to plant a kiss on Rose's forehead. "Have I mentioned how lovely you look in that ensemble?" he asked.

Flustered, Rose paused and glanced down at her pale pink hospital-issue gown. "What?"

Having distracted her from her tirade Will continued: "Ellen and I will be back tomorrow for your surgery. Until then try to behave yourself."

"Behave myself? They're already starving me. Did you see that sorry excuse of a snack?" She pointed to the untouched cup of red gelatin on her over-the-bed table. "If I had known, I'd have finished off the last of the pot roast before we left home."

"You're lucky you got anything once that IV was started," Annie said. "And gelatin is a perfectly acceptable snack for someone who is having surgery tomorrow afternoon."

"Don't remind me." She suddenly became very quiet as Ellen leaned over for a hug.

"I'll see you tomorrow, then?" Rose glanced at Will and Ellen, who now stood near the door.

"We'll be back up here right after the morning chores are done," Will assured her.

Rose sniffed loudly, eyes moist.

"You all right?" Will asked.

"Oh, get going, before I embarrass myself." She shooed the air, waving a tissue.

Ellen grabbed Will's arm and pulled him out the door.

After dimming the lights, Annie sat down in the orange vinyl chair next to the bed. Supposedly the chair's lower half extended, creating a recliner. She assessed the furniture with some doubt. The nurse had brought a pillow and blanket. She'd be fine; after all, she'd slept in much worse conditions and situations the past two years.

Outside the door the orthopedic unit was quiet, with only the occasional squeaky shoe sound of staff passing by or the beep of a patient call light.

Rose's intermittent sniffs and the quiet hum of the IV pump were the only noises inside the room. When Annie reached over to put a tissue box on the bed, Rose took Annie's hand and turned it over.

"I want you to have this. In case I don't make it out of surgery." She dropped a chain into Annie's palm.

Annie unfolded the silver chain gently and held it up to the light. Suspended from the necklace was a delicate silver cross, inlaid with six dark blue stones.

"This is lovely, but I can't take your jewelry."

"I've been meaning to give this to you anyway. It was a present from my momma." She sniffed again, holding a tissue to her reddened nose. "Now seems like the right time."

"Rose. Don't do this to me. You're going to be just fine."

"Did you read that surgical permit? The only situation it didn't cover was a tornado."

"Yes, I know. Nurses call it C.Y.B."

"C.Y.B.?"

"Cover your buns."

Rose laughed, her good spirits returning. "I think they try to scare you to death before they surgerize you, to make sure you're strong enough to handle the real thing."

"There is that," Annie agreed, chuckling at Rose's creative vocabulary. "Besides, if they thought you weren't healthy enough for the procedure they wouldn't be taking the risk."

"Think so?"

"I'm positive."

Rose squeezed Annie's hand again, smiling. "Have I told you lately how proud I am of you?"

Annie smiled back. She wasn't acting like Rose at all. The labile emotions had to be a side effect of the narcotics.

"Well, I am. Sometimes I forget you aren't really my daughter. That makes me sad."

"Oh, Rose. You are the best mother in the world. If you hadn't taken me in and treated me like a daughter, I don't know how I would have gotten by."

"The Lord gave you a good head on your shoulders. You'd have been fine."

"No, really," Annie replied, deadpan. "I was going to run away and become a trapeze artist if things didn't get better."

Rose paused and stared at her. She giggled. "That's a joke, isn't it? You had me there for a minute."

Annie laughed along with Rose.

"I don't want you to leave the ranch, Annie. But

if you have to, if you really feel that the Lord wants you to leave, I'll respect your decision."

"Thank you."

"But have you even considered staying?"

"Rose."

"Is it because of Will?"

"Rose."

"I know you were half in love with him when you left."

Annie sighed. Had her feelings for Will been that transparent? She hoped not. One thing she did know was that it was time to be honest with Rose. She deserved as much.

"Yes, back then I suppose I was half in love with him. But that's the past. I was a kid." She moved her finger along the shiny aluminum bedrail. "Today, I certainly don't know God's plan for *my* life, let alone Will's. Besides, we both know Will says he'll never marry."

"Things change," Rose said.

"I doubt that will change, and if it did, I imagine he'd marry someone Margaret has in mind for him."

Rose snorted.

Annie paused, looking Rose up and down. "Do you remember that nasty Susan Lane my freshman year of high school? That was a hard year for me, and it didn't help that Susan always had an unkind word to say. She always made me feel like an outsider. You told me she was still a sister in the Lord, and I needed to turn the other cheek, every time."

"I remember." The words were a soft response.

"Well, you were right. Eventually she became a good friend."

The room was silent. Finally Rose released a deep sigh.

"I never thought I'd see the day you'd be reminding me of my own words. I suppose I ought to be ashamed of myself."

"No, but maybe you could try being nice to Margaret," Annie suggested. "I mean besides the fact that it's the right thing to do, she is Will's business associate."

"But, Annie, there's so much more going on here."

"What do you mean?"

Rose slapped her hand down on the bed. "Oh, fiddle-faddle."

"Rose?"

"I wish Will wasn't so doggone stubborn. Sometimes the whole situation makes me so mad." Her weathered hands folded the white hospital cotton blanket back and forth in agitation. She let out a breath. "But I suppose that's what makes Will Will."

"What situation?"

"Never mind me. I believe you're right, Annie. We all have to wait on the Lord. Life can seem mighty unfair at times, but He never promised us fair, did He?"

"No," Annie answered, still confused at Rose's outburst. "He promised He'd never leave us."

"And that's the best promise of all." Rose shifted in the bed, repositioning herself.

"Does it hurt? Do you want me to call the nurse?"

"It throbs a little but I'm still riding high on that last shot. Let's wait a while."

"Okay, but let me know. I don't want you in pain."

"I will. Now, you did say you were going to stay until my hip healed, didn't you?"

"Rose, I wouldn't ever leave if you needed me."

"That's what I want to hear. Okay. So tell me about Kenya," Rose said with a yawn.

"What do you want to know?"

"What did you do there? What was it like? The country? The people? The food?"

"That would take me all night."

"I'm not going anywhere."

Annie smiled. "I worked at a government clinic. The first one I was assigned to near Mombasa was closed down. But the next one the program director sent us to was farther from Nairobi, closer to the refugee camps of Dadaab. We had nursing students from Nairobi with us. Sometimes we were asked to visit the refugee camps to assist with vaccinations. The conditions in those camps were deplorable."

"Refugees?"

"From Somalia."

Rose nodded. "Did you see wild animals?"

"Oh, yes. Giraffes are very common. Some of my colleagues and I spent a day at the National Reserve. That was amazing."

"Did you do a lot of evangelizing?"

"To tell you the truth, Rose, most days we were up at dawn and worked until the last patient was seen. We weren't a church or anything. Our mission was to bring God's love through our medical care."

"Ah, Annie, that is the best way."

"That's what I think, too. Besides, once a month we all went down to the mission church close to the city center in Nairobi and attended service and helped out. So I think we covered our bases."

"What are the people like?"

"It's just a different world. People aren't in a rush. They walk for miles just to see the doctor. And they never complain."

Rose made a noise of agreement.

Annie paused. "I love Africa, Rose. It's a beautiful country." She massaged a hangnail. "Funny thing is I discovered I love to travel. It worries me sometimes. Makes me wonder if I'm like my mother and I'll never settle down." She dared a glance up, to gauge the older woman's response.

Rose was asleep, snoring gently.

Just as well. Tonight she really didn't want to hear Rose's opinion on whether she was like Leanne.

Quietly, Annie reached over for the bed controls and turned off the lights. She examined the necklace in her hand. The smooth, worn metal shone in the soft glow of the bed's night-light. She fastened the chain around her neck, placing the cross neatly in the middle of her chest, close to her heart.

Chapter Five

Annie flipped the channels on the television. Will had installed a satellite dish since she'd left. When she realized she'd perused more than a hundred channels in ten minutes, she turned the device off, unwilling to give in to the lure of couch potato technology.

This morning Ellen was at the hospital with Rose. Will had taken off to Tulsa. He'd gone to a medical supply store to buy the safety items Rose's therapist recommended to ensure her smooth transition to home. An elevated toilet seat and safety rails for the shower were the standard equipment Will would install when he returned.

Annie walked through the tidy house and looked around. The place was spotless; the laundry caught up, thanks to Ellen, who had followed Rose's strict instructions and refused to allow Annie to help with chores. It was difficult to get accustomed to being lazy. Ellen had even watered the pumpkin patch and Rose's garden before she left.

She paced and realized she was not accustomed to, nor comfortable with, doing nothing. There wasn't anything on her schedule until tomorrow morning, her "shift" at the hospital.

Tomorrow she'd meet with the physical therapist to again go through the daily home exercise routine once more, though the therapist planned to visit the patient three times a week here at the ranch.

Perhaps her strong desire to get back to her kitchen was inspiration, but Rose's surgical recovery amazed everyone. The only setback had been a temperature spike two nights ago. Dr. Wyatt started her on an antibiotic and increased her respiratory therapy treatments and ambulatory activity. The patient responded immediately.

After a significant amount of cajoling, Dr. Wyatt agreed to allow a Sunday afternoon discharge, but only because Annie was a registered nurse.

Opening cupboards, Annie inspected the kitchen. It had been such a long time since she'd cooked or baked. Knowing Rose, there was probably a good stock of anything needed to bake cookies. She searched the cupboard above the sink for Rose's huge cookbook and found the oversize tome right away. Held together with rubber bands and stuffed with loose scraps of paper, the book held Rose's, Will's and Annie's favorite recipes.

Time for a batch of killer oatmeal cookies, a treat she'd invented in high school. The recipe was handwritten on one of the last blank pages of the book.

Preheating the oven, she gathered the ingredients

and efficiently mixed them in a large yellow bowl, blending them with an ancient wooden spoon.

At the last minute she dug out chocolate chips, hidden in the vegetable drawer of the refrigerator. Rose knew Will would never find them there. He wasn't big on any kind of green vegetable, but he could be counted on to eat the chocolate chips right from the bag.

Annie spooned the dough into small piles and slid the baking sheet onto the oven rack. She'd just rinsed her utensils when the front doorbell rang.

She made her way across the smooth wood floor with care. While she relied on her cane less and less, the trade-off was that her steps were slower. Annie pulled open the door as the impatient buzzer rang yet again.

Margaret Reilly.

Margaret was every inch the sophisticated businesswoman, in black slacks and a pale gray embroidered blouse. Silver hoops dangled at her ears, and her highlighted blond mane was pulled back into a smooth chignon. She'd apparently further accessorized with a foil-covered casserole dish.

A heavy sigh escaped Annie when she remembered what she'd tossed on this morning. Perhaps she should have put on something less casual than her oldest, threadbare jeans and a faded TU Golden Hurricanes jersey.

She stepped back as Margaret swept past her and into the foyer.

"I was beginning to think no one was home," the

older woman remarked with an inquisitive glance around the ranch house.

"I must have missed your phone call."

"Oh, I didn't call." She assessed Annie's attire, leaving Annie no doubt that she looked less than impressive. "I hope I'm not interrupting."

Annie straightened her shirt.

"I brought a little something." The casserole dish was thrust at Annie.

Annie gave an appreciative sniff as she accepted the dish. "This smells amazing."

"Vegetable lasagna."

She peeked beneath the foil and noted the generous mounds of vegetables and cheese. "How thoughtful of you. You'll have to share the recipe."

"I only wish I'd made it. Chef did. I'm terribly busy with KidCare. But I'll get you the recipe."

"You have a chef?"

"Of course. I don't have the luxury of time to cook." She turned her head and inhaled. "Are you making cookies?"

"Yes," Annie said, walking toward the kitchen.

"Let me get that," Margaret said, taking back the casserole.

"Ah, thank you."

"So you bake, too. A regular little Rose, aren't you?"

Had she just been insulted?

"I'm not allowed in our kitchen. Chef would have a fit. Is Will around?"

"He's gone to town."

"Don't you find it a bit awkward with just the two of you here?"

"The two of us?" Annie stared at her a moment, until comprehension dawned. "Rose's sister, Ellen, is staying to help out. But no, it wouldn't be awkward either way."

Margaret digested that information with a slight nod. "Oh, and before I forget, my secretary will be mailing out invitations to the launch party for Sullivan Ranch. This is rather late notice, but it's been difficult to work a party around Will and KidCare's schedule. I hope you're free."

Annie bit back a laugh at the thought that her social calendar was booked. "When is it?"

"A week from Sunday."

"Of course I'll come. Thank you for including me."

"There's someone I'd like you to meet." Margaret glanced at the coffee carafe. "Do you mind if I pour myself a cup?"

"Pardon me, I should have offered." Annie pulled down two mugs and set them on the table along with spoons and the sugar bowl and creamer.

Margaret quickly made herself comfortable.

"Is Rose also invited to the party?" Annie asked, as she poured the coffee.

"The housekeeper?"

"Yes. Rose O'Shea," Annie said.

"Well, of course, I suppose. I mean if that's what Will wants."

The oven timer went off. Irritated, Annie slapped

at the button. She donned mitts to remove the sheet of plump, hot oatmeal cookies from the oven. The sugary aroma filled the kitchen. Still speechless from Margaret's words, she moved them carefully to a cooling rack.

"I really shouldn't," Margaret said, when Annie offered her a cookie. "But they smell delightful."

"Thank you," Annie murmured. She stood at the counter and sipped her coffee.

Margaret finished a dainty bite and wiped her lips with a napkin before she addressed Annie again. "Is Will feeling all right?" she asked. "He's been very preoccupied lately and, well, I'm becoming concerned."

"Preoccupied?" Annie blinked hard. "Rose just had surgery."

"Yes, I know. Oh, pardon me for not inquiring. How is she?"

"Well. She's giving the therapist a hard time about using the walker, which is always a good sign."

"Between you and me, don't you think Will is unusually attached to Rose? I have to admit I find it a strange situation. He is, after all, the owner of Sullivan Ranch and—"

Annie cut her off before she said the words. Words which would no doubt force Annie to lose her temper. "Another cookie?"

"Oh, no, dear. But these are delicious." Margaret leaned forward. "The thing is Annie, Sullivan Ranch and Will are up-and-coming names in Tulsa. They're a brand, so to speak. A brand that KidCare is very effectively marketing. This is an important time for all of us. You know of course that it speaks volumes that Ed and I have taken him under our wing as our protégé."

Annie took a deep, calming breath before she answered. "Yes, and I'm thrilled for him. But then again I'm not involved in your business with Will."

"No, I suppose not, but I had hoped I might get some encouragement from you, as you are Will's little sister, so to speak."

Measuring her words as she measured the dough, Annie prepared another dozen cookies to go into the oven. "Margaret, let's be clear. I am not Will's sister. His friend, yes, but not his sister."

"I didn't mean to insult you. What I meant is that I hoped the two of us might be friends. Especially since Rose is definitely not on my side."

"Side? I didn't realize there were sides. We all want what's best for Will." Annie patted the neat little piles with the back of a spoon. Counting to ten under her breath, she slid two more aluminum trays into the oven, allowing the door to slam closed.

She set the timer and released a small prayer for the Lord to intervene before she said something *Will* would regret. That done, she turned to face Margaret.

"Annie?" Will's voice rang out from the front hall.

Thank You, Lord.

"In the kitchen," she called, as she placed the huge mixing bowl and spoon in the sink and ran water.

"Will," Margaret said. "What a surprise."

He frowned at her comment. "I live here. What brings you out today, Margaret?"

"I brought over a vegetable lasagna casserole. I realize with Rose in the hospital you might be on your own."

Will gave an anorexic smile as he removed his mirrored sunglasses. "Great." He turned to Annie. "I got those safety things for Rose."

"Maybe Margaret has time to give you a hand installing them."

"Pardon me?" Margaret asked, perplexed.

"A raised toilet seat and shower safety rails. I'm not much help with this leg." Annie tapped her left leg.

Margaret stood. "I'd love to, but I have another appointment. Oh, and Will, I'll be by early tomorrow afternoon to direct the caterers and rental people."

"Sounds like a plan," Will said. He led her toward the front hall.

"Goodbye, Annie," Margaret said. "As always, it's been enlightening chatting with you."

"As always," Annie muttered, scrubbing a spatula in the warm soapy dishwater.

The front door closed and she heard Will's footsteps behind her.

"Enlightening? Okay, what did you tell her this time?"

"That if she wanted to get on Rose's good side she better quit calling her the housekeeper."

"Thanks, I've been meaning to—" The timer interrupted him. "Let me get those for you," he said, opening the oven and peeking inside.

"Thanks."

With a finger, Will pushed his black Stetson farther back on his head. When he slid on the bright pink oven mitts and removed the trays Annie was unable to hold back a laugh.

"What's so funny?"

"Not funny. Just cute. The cowboy gets domestic."

He placed the trays on top of the stove.

"Where's a camera when you need one?"

He pulled off the mitts. "Missed your chance. Now nobody will believe you."

"I guess it'll be our little secret."

Will winked and shot her a teasing smile.

She paused, suddenly breathless. Was Will flirting with her? No, she must have imagined that coy expression on his face.

"Shall I heat up that casserole Margaret brought over?" Annie asked, quickly changing the subject.

Will removed the cover of the pan and examined the contents with a sick expression before replacing the foil. "Any of that stew from last night left over?"

"Yes, but what am I supposed to do with the vegetable lasagna?"

"Rose would wash my mouth out with soap if I answered that question. Let's leave the thing for Ellen."

Annie made a small noise of disapproval, then stopped when she realized she sounded just like Rose.

Will reached into the cookie jar.

"Hey, you haven't eaten lunch yet."

Leaning against the counter, he thoughtfully chewed and swallowed. "Nice shirt."

She glanced down. "Thanks."

"You always did make the best oatmeal cookies," he said. "And by the way, you sound just like Rose."

Annie wiped the counter down with force, remembering Margaret's comment. Little Rose.

"Everything okay?" Will asked.

"I'm fine." She tossed the sponge into the dishwater.

"No, really. What's wrong?"

"Nothing," Annie said, drying her hands and tugging the refrigerator door open.

"Nothing?"

"That's what I said."

"Then could you tell me why you just put Rose's cookbook in the refrigerator?"

Annie opened the refrigerator again, discovering he was correct. She snatched the book out and returned it to the cupboard above the sink. "I've got a lot on my mind."

"You know what?" Will dusted crumbs from his hands. "I think you could use a little R & R. You've been at that hospital too many hours, and cooped up in this house even longer."

"You have toilet seats and safety bars to install."

"Come on," he urged, ignoring her comment. "It's time to break out."

She turned to him. "What did you have in mind?"

"Doesn't matter. Your call." Will raised his hands, palms open. "Anything you'd like."

There was no hesitation. "The mall," Annie said.

"What?" He shook his head as though he was hearing things.

"The mall. I want to go to the mall."

"Woodland Hills? That's your idea of a good time?" Will groaned. "You've been in the bush for two years and you want to return to the gathering place of the wild beasts?" He stared at her cane. "What about your leg?"

"I don't care. I want to go shopping." She was thoroughly fed up with looking like—well, like Will Sullivan's little sister.

Will glanced at the clock on the dash as they pulled into the drive of Sullivan Ranch. "Good night. Who would have thought a person could spend five hours shopping?"

"Just making up for lost time."

Will grunted. "No kidding."

"I'm exhausted," Annie said, gathering the cane, her purse and a large, neon-blue shopping bag.

"Need help?" Will asked, as he opened her door and leaned toward her.

"No. I've got it," she said, her voice rising.

Will frowned, puzzled.

"I mean, no thank you. I've got it." She slid out of the truck.

He opened the tailgate and pulled out four large department-store bags. "Lived here all my life and never realized that mall had one hundred and sixty-four stores."

"You counted?"

"Had to do something to pass the time."

"You counted all the stores?"

"I read that on an advertisement while you were trying on shoes for an hour."

"It was not an hour. Besides, when I came out it took me that long to find you."

"You were looking in the wrong places, Annie girl. I was right there all the time." He couldn't hold back a grin.

"Not quite," Annie muttered, her cheeks suddenly touched with pink.

"Sure I was."

"Victoria's Secret? And I could barely drag you away from those sales associates who were quizzing you on your perfume preferences."

Will laughed. "Just being hospitable. If I didn't know better I'd say you sound jealous."

The pink color now spreading across her cheekbones only deepened as Annie opened her mouth and then closed it again. "I... Will Sullivan, you cut that out."

"Didn't they tease you in Africa?" He raised his brows.

When he held the screen open for Annie a fat drop of moisture landed on his arm.

They were both silent, staring at the sky.

"Rain," Annie whispered. She reached out a hand to catch the scattered drops.

Dread settled on Will like a heavy blanket as he willed the sun to reappear.

No. No. It couldn't be raining.

With each passing moment the precipitation increased, small drops turning into a downpour. They stood at the screen solemnly looking out at the landscape.

"How will this affect the program tomorrow?" Annie asked, her voice hushed.

Everything was at stake. Will shook his head, almost afraid to answer, determined to remain calm. "It depends on how long and how hard the storm is."

"The worst-case scenario?"

"Cancellation." He released the breath he'd been holding. *A death knell in his business.* "That means a domino of issues—refunded vendors, rescheduling an already tight calendar. And we'll be eating barbecue at the house until the cows come home."

"Oh, boy." She paused. "Doesn't insurance cover this?"

"I can't afford rain insurance for these small events."

"Oh, Will…" Annie said, her voice trailing off.

Will reined in his fears. "All part of doing business. I just don't have the luxury of a cushion for lost profits this early in the game."

"Then I guess we'd better get some serious prayer in motion."

"As opposed to not serious prayer?"

"Hey, Sullivan. This isn't a joke." She frowned, obviously disappointed in his response. "I can't even count the number of times over the past two years when all I had was prayer to carry me through. I learned to make prayer my first line of defense, not my last."

"Sorry, Annie." He followed her into the kitchen, where she dropped her parcels. "I'm ashamed to say I've been a cynic when it comes to prayer."

"Well, then you're long overdue for a change of heart."

Irritation remained evident as she plopped down into a chair and rummaged in her bags.

"What are you looking for?" he asked.

With a sigh of satisfaction, she finally pulled a candy bar out of a tissue-stuffed bag.

"I have been thinking about this for two years."

Will glanced at the plain milk chocolate, his personal favorite, as Annie slowly peeled back first the paper and then the foil and stared at the smooth bar.

"No chocolate in Kenya?"

"Yes, I could have bought it in Mombasa, but then I'd feel I had to share it with the children at the clinic or shove it all in my mouth before we got back to camp."

"I can see you doing that."

"Don't be silly. Chocolate is to be savored, piece by piece."

"Really?"

"Will, you have no idea what an extreme privilege this represents. An entire bar, all my own."

"So you aren't going to share."

"Not *my* bar." She reached into the bag and pulled out another, handing it to him, then carefully bit off a piece of her own. Moments passed before she spoke. "This chocolate is symbolic."

"What is this? The parable of the chocolate bar?"

Her lips quirked upward. "Not quite."

"Okay, you've got me now. Tell me about the symbolism of chocolate."

"This represents wants." She held up the rest of the bar. "A few precious moments." She snapped her finger. "Gone. There's barely enough nutritional value here to sustain a human."

"You said you had been thinking about one for two years."

"Oh, not that way. It took the attack in Kenya to make me realize how many wants I used to have. I took my life for granted."

Will tore open his chocolate and bit off a large corner. He wasn't into savoring.

"I sound silly," she finally said.

"Not at all. What you experienced in Kenya was life changing. I appreciate that."

"Do you? Then you're probably the only one who does."

"Yeah, well, I know what it's like. You get the curse with the blessing. Sometimes you aren't sure which is which. But the experience changes you. Forever."

She nodded slowly, thoughtfully. "That's it exactly. You can never go back to the person you used to be."

"That person doesn't exist anymore." He stared out the window at the rain.

Were his dreams being washed away with the storm?

Annie sighed. "I really am tired. I'm going to put these things away and rest and pray about that weather."

They reached for the bags at the same time.

"I've got them," she said. "You hauled them all over Woodland Hills Mall. I think I can handle down the hall."

"I'm going to check messages."

A few moments later Annie called out, "I heard a car door slam. Ellen must be back."

"Good, because all of Rose's friends have been calling for an update." The phone began to ring as he spoke. "See what I mean?"

"Want me to grab that?"

"I'm good," he said.

Annie's door closed as he picked up the portable. "Sullivan Ranch."

"This is James Morrow, calling for Anne Harris."

"Annie?"

"Yes. I'm one of the field supervisors from her mission program."

Will released a breath, not wanting to guess what was coming next. He strolled into the living room and out of earshot.

"This is Sullivan Ranch, correct?"

"Yeah, you got the right place."

"Is Anne Harris available?"

"Not right now. She's resting."

"How is she? Everyone is asking about her."

"She's doing as well as can be expected, considering she survived a terrorist attack."

There was a pause from the caller. "May I leave a message?"

"Why don't you try again, maybe next week?" Will clenched his jaw. *Maybe next year.* He knew his anger was misplaced, but the thought of Annie leaving again was making him irrational.

He wasn't ready for her to leave. She'd barely just gotten back.

"Next week?"

"Things are pretty busy here now."

"Could you tell her I called? It's important. We've got all her paperwork for the Mexico trip ready and on hold until she's released from her doctor."

Will's gut took a direct hit, the air whooshing from his lungs. "What?"

"Just have her call me. She has my number."

"You know, your best bet is to call back. Have a good day, Mr. Morrow." Will pressed the disconnect button.

He paced across the living room. Could things get any worse? First the rain, now this. He shook his head; he was ill-prepared for either one.

Will slammed a fist against his palm. Annie's words rang in his ears. *You're long overdue for a change of heart.* What did he need to do to make his prayers heard? "Lord," he said aloud, "I'm sorry. Please forgive me. We've got to talk."

Chapter Six

It didn't take a genius to figure out he had a problem. For one, there were way too many women in his life. That alone was enough to cause any man a severe headache. Then there was the weather.

Rain, rain and more rain.

As the Jeep moved over the bumpy terrain, a drip of water from the soggy canvas roof slipped through a hole and landed with a small splash on Will's face. He swiped at the moisture with the back of his hand.

Things might have fared better had Ed Reilly been around to support him. Will now faced the first big KidCare-sponsored event with Margaret as diva-in-charge, Ellen giving suggestions from the house, and Rose calling in orders from her hospital bed. Annie appeared to be the only normalcy in his life at the moment.

If he wasn't nervous, he ought to be.

Sitting in the Jeep, looking out at the soaked campground, he rubbed the bridge of his nose.

A glance at the sky confirmed his worst fears. Dark clouds still hovered overhead. Should he cancel now or wait until later in the day? What would Ed do?

He stepped out of the vehicle and right into the middle of a large puddle. Pulling his booted foot out, he shook the mud off. "Lord, I need a whole lot of patience today."

Will tried to unlatch the wooden gate, but his fingers refused to cooperate.

His hand trembled.

He stopped and leaned on the gate, breathing slowly, eyes closed. His mind immediately conjured up the word.

Huntington's.

A thread of panic tore through him as he examined his hand, holding the extremity up, using the other hand to steady himself at the wrist. The trembling stopped.

Stop jumping to conclusions.

A hastily eaten piece of toast was breakfast before taking Annie to the hospital at 6:00 a.m. And how much coffee had he downed today? Way too much and it wasn't even noon. *Caffeine overload, pure and simple.*

Time to quit looking for trouble in other places.

Will strode back to the Jeep and opened the glove box where there was a stash of nutrition bars. He pulled one out and grabbed a bottle of water from the backseat.

Eating the bar and washing it down, he rested on

the bumper of his vehicle for a moment as the rain dripped around him.

Too much caffeine. That was all.

His cell phone rang and he pulled the device from his jacket pocket. "Hello."

"Hey, can you use some help?"

He recognized Annie's voice and relaxed. "Where are you?"

"At the house."

"How'd you get back from the hospital?"

"Ellen. After you left, I met with the therapist. About nine o'clock, friends from Rose's bridge club showed up. When they decided they were going to hang out with her most of the day, Ellen and I came back to town. Think you can use a sidekick with a limp?"

"I appreciate the offer, Annie, but there's not much to be done."

"You're not going to give up, are you?"

His jaw clenched. "This isn't giving up. Simply bowing to Mother Nature."

"Canceling?"

"It's not like I want to. Hang on. I'll bring the Jeep to the house."

When he pulled up she was standing under the eaves of the porch waiting. Dressed in old jeans and a hooded sweatshirt that concealed her hair, she played with one of the barn cats who'd taken cover on the porch.

He tooted the horn, and she stepped down and slid into the Jeep.

"Where's your cane?" he asked.

"I'm going without. I have an Ace bandage on the leg for support and I'm feeling good," she barked.

"You sound real good," he said, noting her sharp tone.

"It's barely sprinkling." Her dark eyes pleaded as she spoke.

"Sprinkling doesn't dry up the ground."

"What about hay?"

"No matter how much hay I put down, the fact is, it is still raining."

"Sprinkling."

"Let's drive around the ranch and take a look."

"So what was the plan? I mean, if you weren't going to cancel."

"If it wasn't raining, the night would have started with a little meet and greet. Catered barbecue. A three-piece band for praise and worship and a few scheduled speakers."

"What time?"

"Around six-thirty. Done about ten, ten-thirty."

"Then what?"

He narrowed his eyes as he guided the Jeep over the muddy trail. "Then the group would camp out, using the pup tents and the cabins. They leave in the morning after a short service."

"How were you getting them out here from the road?"

"I've got the two wagons used for hayrides set up with tractors pulling them. The wagons hold about twenty-five to thirty kids each. Moves at a slow clip, but that's a plus on the safety side."

Annie glanced at her watch. "What time is sunset?"

"Around seven-thirty. I had mercury lights installed." He stopped the Jeep and pointed to the lights. "See?"

"You are prepared."

"Hey, I was a kid once. When this was in the planning stages, I sat down and tried to think of all the ways I could get into trouble. That headed off a whole lot of problems right off the bat."

Suddenly her laughter rang out, brightening even the dark day.

"What's so funny about that?"

"You as a kid." Another laugh escaped. "Bet you were the most serious kid in your class."

"I was focused."

Annie smiled, staring out the window.

"What's going on in that head of yours?"

"I'm still thinking about you as a kid."

He shook his head.

"Did you ever wish you had a brother or a sister?"

"Sure. How about you?"

"I always wished for a baby sister." She paused, pensive and faraway for a moment. "But then again, I suppose, if I had a sister, I'd want a brother." A quick grin touched her mouth as she turned toward him. "Do you ever wonder about your mom?"

"What do you mean?" He shifted in his seat,

uncomfortable with the topic, yet knowing that if there was anyone on earth who understood, it was Annie.

"I mean, do you wonder where she is? Why she left?"

Will stiffened. "She left. I don't need to explore the reasons."

"That's so harsh," Annie said, amazement evident on her face.

"Harsh? How so?" He took a calming breath through pursed lips. "The going got tough and she took off. Don't tell me you waste time wondering about your mother."

"I do wonder. I wonder how a woman could walk away. How she could put her needs before that of her child. I think about it all the time," Annie said, sounding perplexed.

Will shook his head. No, he'd decided long ago not to waste time wondering. The facts were plain and simple. His father was handed a death sentence, and his mother walked away when they all needed her most.

"Tell me you never think about whether or not you have other brothers and sisters?" Annie persisted.

"Nope." He shook his head. That was a road he did not go down.

She twisted her face in a frown, obviously dissatisfied with his answer.

"Look, Annie, I don't think it's good to dwell on maybes. I'd go crazy if I did that. So would you." He reached over and touched her shoulder. "We have to be content with the hand life dealt us."

Her steady gaze met his and she looked at him hard. "You really believe that?"

"I do."

The slight smile she gave him said she was not convinced but she'd let the subject drop for now.

He put the vehicle in Reverse and slowly moved toward the tall doors of one of two barns on the ranch. Sliding into Neutral, he pulled up the parking brake.

Annie unbuckled her seat belt. "How many kids did you say you were expecting?"

"The last head count was about sixty."

"Sixty?" She grinned, then tossed back the hood of her sweatshirt as she stepped out of the Jeep. "Sixty?"

"Where are you going? It's raining."

"Barely." She moved to the front of the barn.

Will got out of the Jeep. "Still very wet out here. And every hour it barely rains, the ground gets wetter."

"The cabins are dry."

"Yeah, but that's about all. I've still got a band and caterers I don't want to electrocute."

"Yes. Electrocution is so messy."

He glared.

"Come on, Will. We can't give up. *Think*."

"We?" he asked.

"Yes, we. If you fail, Sullivan Ranch fails and I care too much about both of you to let that happen."

Will looked at the ground, humbled by her words.

"Is the barn watertight?" she asked.

"Yeah. Got a new roof a few months ago. I'm storing the tractors and the wagons we were going to use tonight, riding lawn mowers, tools, along with some old farm equipment."

"So why can't we use the barn? It's big enough. Why, you could hold a wedding in there."

"I just told you. It's full of old farm equip—"

"I heard you. Let's empty the barn."

"Annie, that'll take hours."

"We have hours."

"How are you and I going to haul the contents of that barn by ourselves?"

"We'll toss the stuff on the wagons and move everything to—what about the other barn?"

"That one isn't watertight."

"So we'll cover everything with tarps."

"You can't do that kind of work."

"I've built huts in Kenya. I can do this."

"You weren't recovering from a gunshot wound then."

"Will, I know my limitations," she said. "You'll have to trust me."

He stared at her and then at the barn. Hope like a tiny spark began to grow inside him until he felt its warmth. *Could they make this work?*

Maybe it was time he started trusting, asking for help when needed. Perhaps that realization alone was the answer to those prayers she spoke of. Finally, he pulled out his cell.

"What are you doing?"

"I'm calling Margaret to tell her we're still on. Then I guess I better call Chris to get him out here *after* he stops by the hardware store for tarps, lights and electrical cords."

Annie's eyes lit up. She grinned and launched herself at Will. "Way to go, cowboy."

"Whoa there." Laughing, he caught her in his arms as if it was the most natural thing in the world to be hugging Annie in the rain. "Better save your energy," he said. "We've got a whole lot of work to do."

Somehow it didn't seem like work when you liked what you were doing, when you had a purpose. Annie understood why Will labored such long hours on the ranch, day after day. He loved what he did. There was satisfaction in working hard. It was really no different than nursing.

After shaking straw from her clothes, she stripped off her dirty jeans and stepped in the shower. Despite working on her feet for hours, she was energized. In fact, she felt better than she had since working in Kenya. Useful and productive again.

Needed.

Chris brought a buddy with him, and together the four of them emptied the barn, swept out the floor and laid clean hay where necessary. Then they set up lighting using the ranch's cherry picker.

Annie sneezed. Her allergies seemed to be the only part of her that was balking at the moment.

Satisfied her incision was no worse for the day's

activity, she donned clean gray sweats and white socks, then combed her wet hair, braiding it into a single plait once more.

She headed for the kitchen. Ellen would be home soon, and she didn't want her to have to cook after having spent the day taking care of chores at her own little house in Catoosa.

Annie stood staring into the freezer at the labeled containers.

"Did they answer you yet?"

"What?" She turned and met Will's grin. He looked worse than she had. A film of red dust covered his face, rising to stop just where his hat had protected his head and forehead. Underneath all that grime he wore a grin bigger than she'd ever seen on his face.

Will liked being in control, and today they'd conquered Mother Nature. No small feat. Annie couldn't resist a tender smile.

"Looks like you're having a serious discussion with the contents of that icebox," Will said.

"I'm trying to decide what to fix for a quick meal. But it doesn't look like there's anything fast and easy in here."

"Rose doesn't do fast and easy. You know that. That's why I ordered pizza."

"They don't deliver out here."

"Sure they do, especially when I dangle a fat tip as bait."

Hopeful, she closed the freezer door and assessed him. "Did you really order pizza? *Real* pizza?"

He grinned. "We don't do fake pizza out here."

"Mazzio's?"

"Of course. Two extra large, deep pan. Oh, and Canadian bacon and pineapple for you. Still your favorite?"

"You remembered." She narrowed her eyes. "You're not joking, are you?"

"Annie, I never joke about food."

The front doorbell rang. "See?"

"So fast?"

"Placed the order on my cell after I dropped you off at the house."

"I owe you big-time for this."

"The way I see it, I owe you," Will said. The sincerity of his words reached out to her. Annie's breath caught for a moment.

She followed him to the front door, where he took the boxes from the teenager on the porch. "Thanks for coming all the way out here," Will said. He slid three twenty-dollar bills into the kid's hand. "Keep the change."

"Mister, you can ask for me anytime."

Annie snatched the containers from Will, moving quickly to the kitchen with her prize. She grabbed several cans of root beer and set them on the table.

"I've got to hurry," Will said from behind her. "I have less than thirty minutes before Margaret arrives."

"You wash, I'll get the plates."

Will rolled up his sleeves. "Deal."

Annie placed a stack of napkins beside the plates and looked at Will. "Do we need forks?"

Frowning, he grabbed a dish towel. "For pizza?"

Annie smiled and served herself, then slid the open pizza box across the oak table.

"Do you know how long it's been since I've had pizza?" She picked up a piece of cheese from her pizza and swirled it on her finger before popping it in her mouth. Biting into a slice resulted in a moan of pleasure she was unable to contain.

Will's eyes rounded. "Your pizza must taste lots better than mine."

"Sorry, but this is really incredible."

"Not a problem." He laughed. "Pizza and a floor show."

The doorbell rang again, and Will shoved the last of his slice into his mouth and stood. He stuck his head into the hall and frowned. "She's early."

"Margaret's here already?"

Annie heard the front door swing open.

"You're not dressed." The tone in Margaret's voice as she addressed Will was enough to make Annie want to take cover.

"Well, sure I am. I've got clothes on."

"That isn't what I meant. We agreed that you were going to dress in Western apparel for this event."

Margaret followed Will into the kitchen. She wore a starched white Western blouse with snaps, pink horseshoe yoke and black cord trim. A shiny silver bolo and cord were at her collar. Black creased Levi's and spotless, black leather Western boots with silver tips completed her cowgirl ensemble.

Annie admired the expensive boots, then cringed remembering the amount of mud between here and the barn.

Will glanced down at his jeans and navy T-shirt, just before he grabbed the last slice of pizza from the open box. "Here's a news flash. This is cowboy gear. This is what a down-home boy wears when he's been working his tail off all day emptying a barn. I haven't had time to shower, much less change."

"Uh," Margaret commented, as she passed him. "I believe you. You smell awful."

Will stepped back with a laugh. "Authentic cowboy aroma."

Margaret shuddered. "You realize the caterers will be here in less than an hour and the first buses arrive in an hour and a half?"

"The less talking I do the sooner I'll finish my dinner."

"I hope you'll hurry."

"Sit down and relax. Have some pizza." He pushed open the lid on the second box.

"No, thank you. I can't eat. I'm too stressed. Ed is counting on us, you know."

"What I know is that this is supposed to be fun."

"Fun?" She tossed a smooth, black leather satchel that resembled a saddlebag onto the counter. "Have you any idea what kind of day I've had? The ice-cream machine we rented is malfunctioning, and I've been all over town trying to find another."

"Sorry you had such a rough day, Margaret."

Annie stopped eating stared at him. *Her?* They were the ones who had just spent five hours mucking out a barn.

"So I understand you saved the day, Annie," Margaret commented, acknowledging her presence.

Annie glanced up and gave a quick shrug. She bit off a piece of sausage and cheese.

"She did. I was all set to cancel. If I was smart, I'd put her on the payroll."

The comment caused Margaret to narrow her eyes.

Will gulped down his soda and stood. "I'd better grab that shower. Be right back."

"Anybody home?"

"Rose." Annie nearly choked. She gripped the table for support and stood.

"Rose?" Will asked, his voice reflecting surprise as he moved to the front door.

"No one else but."

"Did you escape or did they discharge you?" Annie called.

Rose walked into the kitchen leaning heavily on an aluminum four-legged walker. "I cut a deal with the doctor."

"Why am I not surprised?" Will said, reappearing in the doorway. A suitcase was under one arm, a large stuffed animal under the other.

"Dr. Wyatt is going out of town tomorrow, and

since my IV is gone there wasn't any good reason for me to spend another sleepless night in that noisy hospital with that awful food."

"Care to explain this deal?" Annie asked.

"The agreement is, she'll do her treatments and exercise at home, and go back to the clinic Monday for a follow-up," answered Ellen, bringing up the rear, balancing two floral arrangements. "Noisy hospital, hmm? The truth of the matter is her card club caused such a ruckus the staff figured it was the only way to get some quiet on that unit. I think the nurses begged the doctor to let her go home."

"Oh, that isn't what happened at all. I promised that head nurse I'd send Will along with a pie come Monday."

"That I might believe," Ellen shot back. "But they're more interested in Will than your pie, which is the only reason they would help you get out."

Annie couldn't help but giggle. When Rose and Ellen joined in the laughter, Will's ears turned a bright shade of red.

"How nice to see you, Rose," Margaret said when things quieted down.

Rose slowly walked over to a straight-backed chair. "Margaret."

Annie coughed loudly at Rose's curt greeting.

"Will, can you hold this chair so it doesn't move, while I try to sit down?" Rose asked, with a quick glance at Annie.

Ellen slipped a foam cushion beneath her sister

before she descended to the chair, and then moved the walker out of the way.

"What are you going to do about this weather?" Rose asked.

"We have a brilliant back-up plan, thanks to Annie," Will said. He glanced at the wall clock. "Holy cow. This boy's got fifteen minutes before the show gets on the road." He bent down to kiss Rose's cheek and ran toward the stairs. "Shower and change. Back in a flash."

"How are you feeling?" Annie asked. "Do we need to fill any prescriptions?"

"We already did that," Rose said. "I'm feeling pretty good. A tad sore where the drain was removed."

"How's the incision look?"

"Oh, it's so pretty. Are we going to compare incisions?" she asked with a sly grin.

"Please, don't," Margaret exclaimed. "I'm rather squeamish."

"We're only joking, Margaret. Honest," Annie said with a wink to Rose. She helped herself to her third piece of pizza. "Pizza?" she offered the sisters.

Ellen shook her head, refusing. "I call dibs on the rest of that vegetable lasagna in the fridge."

"Who made vegetable lasagna?" Rose asked.

"Chef prepared it for Will," Margaret said.

"Will who?" Rose asked.

Annie cleared her throat. "Wasn't that nice of Margaret, Rose?"

Rose looked from Annie to Ellen. "Very nice," she muttered.

"So what's this brilliant plan Will was talking about, Annie?" Ellen asked loudly.

"We cleaned out the big barn," Annie quickly returned.

"I knew there was a good reason I didn't let him tear that building down," Rose said.

"Now tell me about the good stuff. What kind of food are you serving?" Ellen asked Margaret.

Margaret glanced at Rose, hesitating before answering. "Barbecued beef on sourdough buns, baked beans, corn on the cob and brownies. It's not homemade, but the caterers have a good reputation for putting on an excellent spread."

"I may have to sneak down there," Ellen said.

"I'd be glad to bring you up a plate," Margaret said.

"Would you? Rose, too?"

"Of course."

"And what are the plans for breakfast?" Rose queried.

"Bagels, fresh fruit and juices."

"Sounds like KidCare has done a fine job with this program," Rose said.

"Thank you," Margaret replied, obviously pleased at the nod of approval.

So was Annie. She looked up and her glance connected with Rose's. Rose was at least trying.

"What do you think of the changes Will has made, Annie?" Ellen asked.

"They're incredible, and it sounds like this is only the beginning," Annie replied.

"That's right. Ed and I plan to be working with Sullivan Ranch for a long time," Margaret interjected. "We have so many plans for Will."

Rose emitted a strangled sound, her face pinched and eyes wide with a retort she held back. "I'm heading to my room," she announced.

"A fine idea," Ellen said.

Annie stood to help, wondering if Margaret realized how close she'd come to the eye of the storm.

Hands on the walker, Rose raised herself. "You know you don't have to stay tonight, El."

"Getting sick of me?"

"No, but you have things to do."

"What things? Everett is on the road so much I think that husband of mine is closer to that four-wheeler he drives than he is to me. My house gets lonely."

"Well, I appreciate it. Good to know someone's in the room at night. I'm not real good at getting out of the bed yet. Using muscles I didn't know I had."

"I'm happy to stay, so long as you don't snore."

"Snore? I don't snore," Rose retorted with indignant surprise, as she started walking with slow steps.

Ellen laughed.

"Annie, do I snore?" Rose asked.

"I'm staying out of this," Annie said, clearing the table.

Will popped into the kitchen, a black Stetson in

his hand. Still damp from the shower, his dark hair glistened. He had changed into a pristine, white Western shirt that emphasized the breadth of his shoulders.

"Woo-hoo. Aren't you one handsome cowboy?" Rose commented.

"Thank you."

Very handsome, Annie silently concurred, tamping down the flutters of her heart. Will Sullivan always managed to be the handsomest cowboy in any room.

Margaret slid elegantly from her chair and stood. "I have your name tag."

"Name tag?" He frowned at the silver clip bar.

"So they know we're staff from KidCare."

Will took the tag from Margaret and turned to Annie. "Did you see the first-aid kits I brought in?"

She nodded toward the kitchen counter.

"Those work?"

"Perfect. I'm all set if you need me."

"Great. I guess we're ready."

"Good luck tonight," Annie said to both of them.

"This is pretty exciting," Ellen chimed in. "I think we need a prayer to launch Will's new venture."

"Pray fast," Rose said. "I'm going to need to sit in a minute."

Will took Margaret's hand and then Annie's. They in turn clasped the hands of Rose and Ellen.

"Lord," Rose prayed, head bowed and eyes closed,

"thank You for giving Will this opportunity to expand Sullivan Ranch. Bless tonight's event and keep everyone safe, and may Your name be glorified this evening. Amen."

"Amen to that," Will said. "Let the games begin."

Chapter Seven

"Sullivan Ranch and KidCare are quite a team," Margaret said, while Will loaded the last of her supplies into the backseat of her cream-colored Mercedes. He closed the door and handed her the keys.

"Aren't we?" she persisted, slipping the keys into her purse on the top of the car.

Will nodded in agreement, wary of where the conversation was going.

June bugs drawn by the overhead mercury lights danced around them. Will swatted the insects away with a sweep of his hat.

"And it isn't just the ranch, Will," Margaret said. "It's you. I insisted to Ed that you were the right man for the job. You know, we both feel close to you, like you're our own son."

Will said nothing, not wanting to offend Margaret or Ed. Fact was he wasn't looking for adoption. Merely a business partner, and a temporary one at that.

Margaret continued. "Why, with Ed's grooming, you're going to be important in this community in no time."

He rubbed his fingers over the smooth surface of his Stetson. "Being important isn't real high on my list."

"Nonetheless," she continued, slapping at a mosquito. "Sullivan Ranch is already getting enormous publicity. In fact, did I tell you we had calls asking if you'd participate in a bachelor auction?"

"No way."

"Yes. Really."

"No. I mean there is no way I am doing anything like that."

"Why not? Ryan Jones is going to. It's for Children's Hospital."

"That's Jones's business."

"But—"

"No, Margaret. Ask me for a donation, ask me to hold a fundraiser at the ranch, but don't ask me to exploit myself and compromise my privacy."

"We can discuss it another time."

Will shook his head. He was too tired to argue. He'd deal directly with Ed next week, and nip this nonsense right in the horse's behind.

Margaret perked up. "I'm going to call Ed tonight and give him a full report. Everything went extremely well. You saved a potentially disastrous situation."

"Annie did that. She was an answer to a prayer, you might say." He smiled, remembering Annie's comment about serious prayer. Sure, it had stopped raining eventually, but since the ground remained sloppy, using the barn was the best solution all the way around.

"Annie had the idea but it was *you* who implemented the plan."

"Ah, thanks. You know, there is one thing. I'd like a copy of the liability releases and contact information to be on file at the ranch before the next program."

Margaret stiffened. "That was a communication error. My assistant didn't understand that KidCare was partnering with Sullivan Ranch. I have them at the office if we really need them."

"Better to have them here in case there is a problem during the night."

"Of course. I'll take care of it immediately." She reached into her purse and pulled out a Black-Berry, quickly inserting a note. "The next KidCare project isn't until Friday, correct? The hot dog roast event."

"Yeah, the next two Fridays are pretty much the same—hayrides, weenie roast and marshmallows round the campfire. And I have a few projects of my own going on."

"You're booking your own programs?"

"I have bills to pay."

That was an understatement. While the new venture promised to generate revenue, at this point future business didn't balance out the considerable new monthly debt he was incurring today. There were part-time employees to pay, as well as continued upgrades and plain old maintenance to the ranch.

"You know Ed and I have said over and over that he'd be glad to underwrite you."

"This is Sullivan Ranch. It's been an independent operation for four generations. I intend to keep it that way."

The grip on his hat tightened. *If he needed financing he'd take the problem to the bank.* He wasn't going to be obligated to KidCare except within the parameters of their current working contract.

"You know it takes time to build your base of customers. But by next summer you'll be booked solid with KidCare projects," Margaret said.

"I understand that. But I have to do what I can for the ranch now. That includes bringing in my own clientele if and when I can."

"What do you have scheduled this week?"

"The cabins are booked for a three-day family reunion. Also have a party coming down for group riding lessons. Early next week a women's club is scheduled for a two-day retreat."

"I'm sure that's fine, as long as it doesn't interfere with your big programs with KidCare."

"I wasn't exactly asking your permission, Margaret."

She inhaled sharply. "I'm simply protecting our interests at KidCare. We don't want any scheduling conflicts, now do we?"

"Not going to happen." He might not have a personal assistant at his beck and call, but he had everything he needed on a spreadsheet in his laptop.

"I think it would be prudent to sit down and coordinate our calendars. How about Monday? You could come out to the house. Ed would love a personal update."

Will shook his head. Yeah, that was just what he needed, Margaret having his every move for the next six months on her BlackBerry. He made a noise of regret. "Thanks, but that won't work. Next week is packed. Rose has to go into town for her post-op checkup. I think Annie has a doctor visit coming up soon."

Too bad he couldn't quite remember when that was.

"I see. Well, I hope you aren't overextending yourself." She crossed her arms and tapped her boot on the gravel drive. "Your KidCare duties *must* come first."

Will bit back a wave of irritation. "Margaret, I have it under control."

"Is the launch party Sunday night on your schedule? I planned the entire party around your KidCare schedule."

"I'll be there."

"You're sure?"

"I said I'll be there, Margaret."

She eased up, a small smile appearing. "I'm looking forward to this get-together."

"Did Chris and Joanie LaFarge confirm?"

"Yes, and so did Ryan Jones. I can't wait to introduce him to Annie. I know they're going to click. They have so much in common."

"Annie and Doc Jones?" Why did that idea sour his stomach? He shoved back his Stetson and slid his hands in his pockets. "Like what?"

"Well, they're both in the medical profession."

"He's a vet."

"He's a doctor of veterinary medicine. They're both so much alike." She gave a satisfied smile.

"Alike? How do you figure? Jones is rich and Annie is just…Annie."

Margaret ignored his comment. "Did you know Ryan did a medical-missions stint a few years ago?"

"Where? At the country club?"

"No, in Mexico."

Will stiffened. Great. Just what he needed, every corner he turned someone was bring up Mexico.

"Besides, their personalities mesh. Annie is vivacious and Ryan is extremely outgoing."

Will groaned. "Outgoing? Jones is a rodeo clown."

"You're such a pessimist. I have a hunch they are going to hit it off."

"I s'pose." What he really supposed was that Margaret was a terminal matchmaker.

"Well, I guess I had better get going. I have to be back early in the morning."

"That isn't necessary. I can serve breakfast just fine."

"Oh, no. Sullivan Ranch and KidCare are partners. I wouldn't think of abandoning you."

"Suit yourself, Margaret, but it's only bagels. Even I can handle that." He paused. "You know, I'm wondering why we use a caterer for breakfast if it isn't a hot meal."

"Because KidCare always negotiates with the caterers for these projects."

"Seems to me 'always' isn't a good enough reason. I'll work up some comparisons and see what the numbers say."

"Ed will not be pleased to hear that."

Will glanced at his watch. "Sure is getting late. I'm thinking we can review this later."

"Hey, wake up." Will bent over Annie's sleeping form and gently shook her shoulder. She shifted slightly on the love seat and drew the afghan closer.

"Annie."

"Go away," she said, swatting at his hand. "I don't work today. Umbala is opening the clinic this morning."

"Annie. Come on. It's Will. Wake up."

"Huh?" She blinked and rolled to her back. Eyes wide, she stared, not really seeing him at all.

"You were hollering in your sleep."

"What did I say?"

"I couldn't make it out. You yelled something in another language."

Annie straightened her twisted sweatshirt and looked around. A lock of hair had come loose from her braid, and she pushed the strand back as she struggled to sit up. Her face bore a red crease line from the corded sofa pillow. "Did I wake Rose and Ellen?"

"I don't think so." He reached to turn on the lamp.

"No," she said, her hand on his sleeve.

The room was silent except for the rhythmic ticking of the grandmother clock on the mantel.

"It was so real," she whispered, pain and fear lacing her voice.

"What?"

"The clinic. I was at the clinic. They had rifles." Her eyes became huge dark orbs as she spoke. "Windows broken. Glass everywhere." She sucked in a breath. "All we could do was run." Annie paused, brows furrowed, her face a mask of fear.

Will hesitated to speak, sensing there was more to come. The hairs on his neck prickled in the stillness of the dark room.

"I grabbed the boy. He was running behind his mother. She held the baby." Annie stopped speaking for a moment, sucked in a breath and then went on, her words slow, thick and measured. "A rock. I flew across the dirt." Again she paused. "The child was under me when the rifle…"

Will's body stiffened in sudden shock. She'd been so close to death. So close.

"My leg was on fire."

The minutes stretched. She sniffed the air as though she could still smell the burned flesh and gunpowder. Suddenly she shivered, wrapping her arms around herself.

"What is it?" he asked, pulling the quilt from the back of the couch and covering her thin shoulders.

Her gaze pinned him as she began to rock back and forth. "The mother," she breathed. "She died. Right in my arms."

"I am so sorry, Annie."

Annie stilled. Silent tears slipped from her eyes, trailing slowly down her face. "Will, she had her whole life in front of her. Two children. A future. She died protecting her babies."

Will sat down on the couch and leaned Annie against his chest holding her as she cried.

The first tears he'd ever seen Annie Harris cry.

She was such a sprite. While her tears were noiseless, his heart ached loudly for her grief.

When she finished, he still held her, until all that remained was the deep, shuddering breaths that continued for several more minutes.

"I've been thinking about death a lot lately," she whispered, her words warm against his shirt.

"Now why would you do that?" he asked.

"Because I'm alive."

"Ah, Annie. That is in God's hands."

"Yes, but there has to be a reason."

"Yeah. I used to think there had to be a reason for everything."

Leaning away from his embrace, she sniffed and wiped her face with the back of a hand.

"You've been awfully philosophical lately," he said.

"Have I?" She pulled her knees to her chest. "I suppose so. I've spent my whole life not thinking, avoiding thinking. Kenya has made me realize that God has something for me. I can't be afraid anymore."

"I can't see you being afraid of anything."

"But I have been. All my life, I've been afraid."

"Afraid of what?"

"Lots of things."

Will frowned.

"Mostly afraid that I'll become be like my mother."

"Your mother?" he asked, confused. "Annie, you are nothing like your mother. Anyone can see that."

"I'm not so sure," she answered.

"Besides, we all have fears," Will said.

"Yes, but when they keep us from living the life the Lord wants for us, fear owns us and we aren't living." Her gaze connected with his. "Don't you see, Will? There is no in-between. There's life and there's death."

"What about those times when life becomes more difficult than death? Does that qualify as in-between?"

She looked up at him, brows knitted. "I don't understand."

His mind took him to the last tortuous months his father was alive, and he let out a deep breath. "My father suffered more than anyone ought to have to suffer."

"He was in pain?"

"No, not that kind of suffering. His body betrayed him."

Her hand reached out to clasp his. He accepted the strength she offered.

"I'm so sorry."

"No one knew but Rose and his doctor. And Pastor Jameson." Will gave a half laugh. "Dad wasn't going to let the pastor in the house. But Pastor Jameson is almost as stubborn as my father. He came, invited or not, once a week for years."

They were silent, Annie gripping his hand in the dark room. He had to admit, it was a relief to share those things that stayed bottled up inside him for too long. Share with someone who had no expectations, no judgments, but merely listened.

Annie released a sound of weariness. "Oh, Will. I don't know what to say. I thought I had it all figured out."

"Hey, you don't have to say anything. And you sure don't have to figure it all out tonight."

"That's good." She gave a tremulous smile. "What time is it anyhow?"

"Nearly midnight."

"Are your kids settled down?"

"Yeah, most of them are asleep. I checked in with the camp leader. Margaret just left. She'll be back in the morning."

"How did it go?"

"I think we can call our first project a success."

"Congratulations."

"I'm real glad you're smarter than I am. The barn saved the situation."

"I'm not smarter. I've lived on my toes all my life. Believe me, I've cultivated the art of improvisation."

"Lucky for me, I'd say."

Annie smiled.

"I'm going to put up a lean-to for the wagons, permanently get rid of that old equipment and do a little work on that barn."

"What are you thinking?" Annie asked, her eyes bright with excitement.

"Fix up part of the floor to start. Good to have the barn properly prepared when we need it as a backup. Who knows? Might come in handy for a barn dance, or a concert sometime."

"Or a wedding."

"I guess."

"You could put a first-aid station out there."

"Absolutely."

"A refrigerator and big freezer might be a good idea."

"Great minds. I was figuring maybe I could forget the caterer on some of those small projects. You know the ones where all we're doing is supervising cookouts. Save me some cash and time if I can buy in bulk. Soda, juice, hot dogs and buns." He rubbed the bridge of his nose and released a noise of pain. "I'll have to check the details on my permits."

"Permits?"

"Annie, I've got permits coming and going around this place. I can't scratch my nose without a permit."

She laughed.

The mantel clock began to chime.

"You better get some sleep," Annie said.

"I will. Need to wind down a bit first. What about you?"

"Going to bed." She stood and stretched. "I'm sore all over."

"You ought to be after all the work you did today." He folded the afghan while Annie arranged the quilt on the back of the love seat. Turning, Will bumped right into Annie. The sofa pillow tumbled from her hands.

"Oh, sorry," he said with a chuckle. "I almost knocked you over."

She grabbed the pillow and threw it at him. "Watch it there, cowboy."

When he returned the favor, tossing the pillow back, she ducked. The pillow and a picture frame on the coffee table sailed through the air.

They both stood still as the frame clattered to the floor. Will glanced from Annie to the upstairs hallway.

"You are such a troublemaker," he whispered.

"But I'm your favorite troublemaker." She giggled, then covered her mouth with a hand.

He smiled at the sparkle in her dark eyes and the dimple in her left cheek as she fought back laughter. Not just any sprite. Annie was an endearingly lovely sprite. "Yeah," he breathed softly. "You are."

They stared at each other for a moment before Annie cleared her throat. "Um, well, I better get to bed. Night, Will."

"Night, Annie."

"And, Will?"

"Hmm?"

"Thank you."

He shook his head. "No, Annie. Thank *you*."

Chapter Eight

Annie could hear Ellen and Rose bantering in the kitchen long before she even reached the doorway.

"I hope you aren't planning on church this morning," Ellen remarked.

"There's no way I'm ready to sit that long," Rose replied. "I think it's best I stay home a week or two. We'll see how I'm feeling after that. Besides, that associate pastor is preaching this morning. He's a mite long-winded."

"You're being very charitable, sister. He's *very* long-winded."

"Oh, well. He's got a lot to say, and he only gets a captive audience twice a year when Pastor Jameson is on vacation."

Ellen chuckled.

"Will just finished getting the last of those kids out of here, so he's going to the late service."

"How'd the program go last night?" Ellen asked. "I didn't hear any explosions, and the fire department wasn't called, so I assume there were no problems."

"Will seemed pleased," Rose answered. "He said the only glitch was a kid who wandered off to use the bathrooms and somehow managed to get himself lost."

"Oh, no."

"Will had everything under control in no time."

"Annie going to the late service?" Ellen asked.

"Yes, she's going to help in the nursery in my place."

"She's a good girl, that Annie."

"She sure is, isn't she? And she loves babies. Even if she won't admit it. Why don't you go ahead with her and Will, El?"

"I'm not leaving you alone in this house."

"I'll be fine by myself."

"Ha. That's how you broke your hip in the first place."

"Did I hear my name?" Annie asked, as she stepped into the kitchen.

"My. My. My. Don't you look sophis-tee-cated," Ellen said, looking up from the *Granby Reporter*. She took off her bifocals and stood, circling Annie.

"Me? Sophisticated?" Annie doubted that, but the thought boosted her nevertheless.

"You're hardly limping at all," Rose observed, sipping her coffee.

Annie glanced down at her leg. "Does the bandage look silly with hose? I didn't want the incision showing."

"Hardly noticed," Rose answered. "Where did you get that pretty suit? That teal color flatters you."

"While you were in the hospital Will took me to the mall."

Rose cocked her head to one side and gave it a slight shake, causing the bun on top to wobble. "Good night. I'm going to have to have my hearing checked. Yesterday I heard you say Margaret brought Will vegetable lasagna and just now I thought I heard you say he went shopping at the mall."

Annie giggled. "No. He only drove me there and then followed me around carrying my bags. I'm sure he was feeling sorry for me."

"Will? Will Sullivan?" Rose asked.

"Yes." Annie paused. "Our Will."

"Did he pretend he wasn't with you, like he did when I made him take you shopping when you were in high school?"

"Of course not." Annie laughed. She'd forgotten about that. "But don't say anything or he might get cold feet," she continued in hushed tones. "He's promised to take me back. I need a new dress for Margaret's party."

"Awfully nice of Margaret to include you, too, Rose," Ellen said.

"Oh, go on with you. I'm not going. That's way past my bedtime. But it does make me wonder what Margaret is up to," Rose said.

"Rose," Annie chided.

"We'll expect a full report when you get home," Ellen said.

"Yep," Rose agreed. "Just the important stuff—clothes, food, a rundown on the Reilly home. Oh, and the guest list." She glanced at Ellen for confirmation.

"I should take a notepad, then?"

"Good idea," Rose said.

Annie wasn't clear why she'd gotten a personal invitation to Margaret's party, either, but she wasn't going to refuse an opportunity to peek into the other woman's world. She admitted to a healthy curiosity that came from years of living with Rose.

Will strode into the kitchen and headed straight for the coffeepot. "Looks like you're ready."

"Thanks. You look nice, too," Annie said, assessing his dark blue, Sunday-go-to-church shirt and tie.

She held back a sigh as she glanced at his profile. Life would have been a lot simpler if Will wasn't so attractive.

"Now, Annie, you know you always look nice. Do I have to remind you every time?"

"What a sweet talker you are, Will. No wonder women hang on your every word," Annie replied.

Will glared at her over the rim of his cup. "Don't you know you're supposed to rest from harassing me on the Lord's day?"

Annie pondered that for a moment, opened her mouth and then closed it again. He had a point. She grabbed her purse and Bible from the counter. "Ready?"

Will arched his brows. "Oh, boy. Now I'm in

trouble. No response from my favorite sparring partner."

"Serves you right," Rose said. "You two going to lunch afterward?"

"That work for you?" he asked Annie.

"Yes," Annie replied. "Unless you'd rather we came right home?" She looked to Rose.

"And break tradition? No way."

"I'll take her to your favorite restaurant and we'll keep a chair empty in your honor."

"Tell Stella hello."

"Stella?" Annie asked.

"Her waitress," Will said, downing the last dregs.

"I see."

"Should we bring you something back?" Will asked. "How about some of that famous bread pudding for each of you ladies?"

"Would you?" Rose smiled.

"Consider it done," he answered. "Now be good and catch a nap before we get back."

"Nap? I'm much too young for as many naps as you think I need," Rose protested.

Will greeted familiar faces as he moved down the children's corridor. He'd never been down in this area of the church building and was at a loss as to Annie's whereabouts. At each doorway he peeked in his head, meeting with no success. The farther down the long carpeted hall he strolled, the stronger the scent of baby powder became.

"Hey, Will."

"Chris." He greeted the vet tech and his wife, Joanie. "That your newest addition?" Will asked, noting the baby cradled in Joanie's arms. She unfolded the blanket to show off her bundle, a small infant sleeping peacefully. Tufts of black hair stood up, a stark contrast to the pale pink skin.

"Boy, you lucked out, Chris. That baby boy is beautiful. He doesn't look a thing like you."

Joanie burst out laughing as Chris gave Will a mock cuff to the arm. "Keep it up, buddy. Wait until you have your first. I'm going to get even."

"Ha. That'll be the day. I'm liking this footloose stuff."

"Oh, sure," Chris replied. "But you know what they say, the bigger they are the harder they fall. And, Will, you're about as big a joker as they come, next to Doc Jones, that is."

The baby began to make small noises of dissent as Will and Chris razzed each other.

"Uh-oh, you scared him," Chris said.

"It was you," Will said. "Just point me to the nursery, wise guy."

"Which nursery?" Both Joanie and Chris looked at each other.

"There's more than one?"

"There are several, you greenhorn," Chris said. "What are you doing down Baby Boulevard anyhow?"

"I'm picking up Annie. She's doing duty for Rose."

"How's Rose feeling?" Joanie asked, moving the baby to her shoulder and rocking gently.

"Bouncing back. She's almost up to par."

"Glad to hear that. So it would be okay to stop by the house sometime after Chris and I feed the horses?"

"Sure. She'd love company." Will paused. "Who watches Chris Junior, here, while you two are out at the ranch?"

"My mother lives with us since my dad died."

Will nodded. "Have to have you all over for dinner sometime soon."

"Will, you're starting to sound domestic," Joanie mused.

"Domestic?" He narrowed his eyes. "Maybe you're right. Scratch that." He stuck his hands in his pockets, threw back his chest and gave a swagger. "Chris, what say I meet you down at the Blue Moon and we ride that mechanical bull?"

Chris laughed.

"Very funny," Joanie said drily. "We'd love to come over some time. Maybe bring the baby and my mother, too."

"Good. Rose is a touch claustrophobic. Do her good to visit with the baby and your mom."

"Mom would love that," Joanie said.

"Okay, I'll check with Rose and let you know." As he set off down another corridor, he called over his shoulder. "See you guys Monday."

"Will?" Joanie called.

He turned.

"The nursery you're looking for is the last door at the end on the right." She pointed in the opposite direction he had headed.

"Thanks."

He strolled to the end of the hall and stopped at the big glass picture window, where he spotted Annie seated in a huge oak rocker. She'd taken off her jacket, and the tiniest baby he'd ever seen was nestled on her shoulder, sleeping against her white blouse. Like a satin curtain, Annie's dark hair framed her and the child. When she pushed the strands back over her shoulder with a free hand, Will's heart tripped at the picture they made.

Annie was meant to be a mother and she'd be a wonderful mother. Yes, this was God's big plan for Annie. No doubt considering her childhood, the Lord would have His hands full convincing her.

Mesmerized, he couldn't pull his gaze from the window. As the thought that this was what Annie needed sunk in so did the realization that he'd never be a man in the running to give it to her.

He'd never have children.

The devastating emotional punch hurt as though a physical pain.

Never.

Couldn't risk passing on the gene.

He was the last of the Sullivans. Four generations of only children. From the back of his thoughts the word *adopt* settle into his consciousness. Adopt? Sure, his own father was adopted.

He could adopt.

No.

What was he thinking? The disease. He might not be around long enough to see a child of his marry, just like his dad.

Maybe you don't have the disease, his rational side shot back.

And perhaps Annie was right. If he didn't live each day, then he was already dying from Huntington's—dying, whether he had the disease or not.

Will's hands clenched at his sides. He moved to walk away from the viewing window but Annie's glance caught his. Her mouth curved into the sweetest smile. A smile that told him she was receiving as much as she was giving from her duty in the nursery. She fairly glowed inside and out.

His breath caught in his chest.

Gently, she lifted and cradled the small body, setting the baby down in a nearby crib. She put on her jacket and came out into the hallway. Her hair was stuck inside the fabric. It seemed only natural for Will to reach forward and gently tug the strands free from her collar. Their fingers touched and she pulled away quickly.

He frowned, confused at her response.

"Thank you," she said, shyly ducking her head.

"You like the nursery," Will said. The words were a statement. It seemed all too obvious.

"You know what? I do. The babies are all so adorable," she murmured, a tremor of longing in her voice. "I felt like a little girl playing house." Her gaze met his. "Silly, huh?"

"No," he murmured.

"Are you all right?"

"Hungry."

Annie nodded.

"Sorry you missed the service."

"They pipe it into the nursery. Actually, I only missed half. I left after announcements. You just didn't notice because you were in your happy place."

"I did too notice, and I wasn't daydreaming." He glanced around the church lobby.

"What are you looking for?"

"Margaret wanted me to introduce you to Doc Jones."

"Doc Jones?"

"Ryan Jones, the vet."

"Do I have a sick animal that I don't know about?"

"She's trying to fix you up."

"With a puppy?"

"No. Margaret has some crazy idea you and Doc Jones would be a perfect match."

Annie's eyes fired up, gold sparks in the dark pupils as she digested his words. "She told me she wanted me to meet a friend of hers. Why do I think Margaret has an ulterior motive here?"

"Huh?"

She started off toward the glass doors in a huff.

"Hey, I don't get it. What's going on?" he called after her retreating form.

"Never mind. What's going on here is far too complicated for a cowboy to figure out."

"Darn straight," Will said, scratching his head.

He'd told Margaret right off he didn't think it was a good idea. Besides, everyone knew Jones had never gotten over his fiancée jilting him. Now he'd gotten Annie all irritated and prickly.

What had he said wrong?

Women. Go figure.

"So, Doc Jones is my age?" Annie asked, when Will caught up with her. "I assumed anyone called Doc must be old enough to be my grandfather."

"He went to high school with me."

"That's pretty old."

"It's still Sunday," he warned as he held open the door.

Her lips twitched but she didn't say anything as they left the church.

When they passed a huge navy car in the parking lot, Will stopped and hunkered down, inspecting the tires.

"Looks like Ms. Parson has a flat."

"Ms. Parson? Why does that name sound familiar?"

"Because she's been the town librarian for over one hundred years."

Annie laughed. "No exaggerating on your part, right?"

"It's true. She finally retired last year. Only because she was too busy to run the library anymore."

"How do you know this is her car?"

"Who else in this town owns an '81 Caddy in mint condition?"

"That's a lot of car for a woman who's been around over a one hundred years."

"Yeah, it is. This car gets better care than my truck," Will stated, his tone reverent.

"Oh, I find that a little hard to believe," Annie said, glancing over at the immaculate black pickup.

He ignored the pointed sarcasm in her voice. "This baby isn't out of the garage long enough to gather dust." He ran a finger lightly over the gleaming chrome bumper and held it up. "Spotless. She only drives into town and back. And I don't mean into Tulsa."

"I'm impressed. I'm impressed," Annie said. "So are we going to wait here, or do you want to go find her?"

"No, she'll be along soon. I saw her coming out of the service. She's wearing a red and white polka-dot dress."

"Is this some sort of Sullivan joke?"

"Think I'd make something like that up? When she comes out I'll let her sit in the truck with you while I change the flat. Sound okay?"

"Will, you aren't going to get a frail, tiny, little, old lady up into the cab of your big pickup."

"You got any bright ideas?"

"I'll help her back to the church. They have those comfortable chairs outside the bookstore, near the lobby. We'll wait for you there."

"Good idea," Will said as he removed his suit coat. "Here she comes."

Annie turned and blinked. The five-foot-nothing woman striding toward them was no little old lady. Her short gleaming silver curls bounced as she marched with purpose across the blacktop, carried by bright red pumps. A red leather handbag swung at her side.

"Do you need a ride home, son?" she addressed Will, as she approached.

"No, ma'am. Ms. Parson, I'm Will Sullivan."

"Selling something?"

"Sullivan. Will Sullivan," he repeated slowly and louder than usual.

"Sullivan? Why didn't you say so? You know I was good friends with your daddy and your granddaddy."

"Yes, ma'am, I know."

"So, how are you?"

"Fine, ma'am."

"This must be your wife." She reached out and took Annie's hand giving her a thorough handshake. "Lulu Parson. Delighted to meet you."

Will's neck was pink with embarrassment when Annie turned back to him.

"How's Rose? I heard she had a spill."

"Much better, thank you," Will said.

"When she heals you bring her to my yoga class. That'll keep those bones flexible."

"You take yoga?" Annie asked. Now she *was* impressed.

"I teach yoga. Two classes a week at the Y. Come on over, I'll get you a discount. Bring your husband. We need a few more men."

Will cleared his throat and bit his lip.

"Sorry. I'm jabbering again. Get in. I'm happy to give you a ride. Let your wife ride up front with me."

"Ma'am. Your tire is flat."

"Hat? My hat?" She reached up and patted her head. "I didn't wear a hat today."

Will pointed to the tire.

"Why, that tire is flat."

"Yes, ma'am."

"Thank you for noticing, son." She inserted the key in the trunk. "I'll just have to change that, won't I?"

"May I do that for you?"

"That isn't necessary." She pulled off her white gloves one at a time.

"Ms. Parson, my daddy would have tanned my hide if he ever knew I had let a lady change her own flat tire," Will argued.

Hands on hips, Lulu looked him up and down. "Well, I suppose when you put it that way." She took Annie's arm. "Your wife and I will wait in the lobby and chat a bit."

Annie grinned as the "little old lady" led her off to the church.

"Ah. Cold hands," Rose said with a shiver.

"Oh, sorry," Annie replied, warming her palms

with a quick friction rub against the coverlet on Rose's bed. "That better?" she asked, holding Rose's leg again.

"Yes, thank you."

"Slowly, now," Annie cautioned, elevating Rose's left leg to begin the first set of exercises. "No extra points for finishing early."

Rose glanced at her watch. "My soap opera comes on at three. Today we find out if Lance is still alive, when Marla and Jack are going to get married, and who stole Pammy's baby."

Annie tried not to laugh. "No talking. Concentrate on the muscles in your leg. Isolate them."

They worked silently for the count of eight, then switched legs.

"Seven. And eight." Annie stopped. "Nice job. By the end of next week, you'll be doing the exercises all by yourself."

"Oh, no, I won't. I just got home. It's way too early to even think about doing them by myself."

"I'm not buying that baloney," Annie said.

"Well, what would you buy?"

Annie did laugh then. "I didn't say you had to do them alone. I'll be standing right here with you as you do the exercises yourself. That better?"

Rose nodded. "Good. For a minute there I thought you were trying to tell me you were leaving already. Don't think I haven't noticed you haven't unpacked your trunk yet."

"Trust me. You'll be the first to know when I'm leaving. This isn't about me, Rose. You have to do as much for yourself as you can now, so you can be out harvesting that garden at the end of summer and making pies for the fall festival."

"Oh, sure, go ahead and make sense. You never play fair. Reality always has to rear its ugly head."

"Are you breathing in and out with each repetition, like I showed you?" Annie asked.

"Why, of course I am."

"That can't be easy with all the talking you're doing," Annie observed.

Rose released a breath, silently counting under her breath.

"Try to lift your leg by yourself, this set," Annie directed.

"Why is it the older I get the harder it is to lift my leg?" Rose asked. "I feel like an old dog." She groaned and slowly raised her affected leg.

"Concentrate on the exercises, and then when you get stronger we'll start walking together. Maybe you and I will get a membership at the Y. Oh, that reminds me. I met Lulu Parson on Sunday."

Rose choked out a laugh. "How could you let a thing like that slip your mind? You don't just meet Lulu. She's a small tornado."

Annie laughed. "She invited us to her yoga class."

"Ha. That'll be the day I get into one of those leotard and thong getups." Rose hooted loudly.

"The last time I checked, leotards and a thong were not the required uniform for yoga. And I haven't been gone that long."

"Maybe not for a young one like you, but around my age group they get a little crazy. Classes at the Y are like Friday night at the Blue Moon Tavern for some of those old gals. They wear more makeup and jewelry to stretch their gluteus muscles than they do for church. Doing their best to catch the attention of some old geezer in sweatpants."

"Thank you. That's quite a visual you just painted for me." Annie shook her head. "So what's wrong with love in your prime?"

"Love? True love only comes once in your life. Those gals aren't looking for love—they're just looking to supplement their pension checks."

"Oh, my, Rose. I never realized you were so cynical."

"Don't get me started."

Annie raised her brows. She had no idea the topic would raise such a passionate response.

Rose glanced at the clock again. "Ten minutes until my show starts."

"Okay, let's do a little gentle range of motion." Annie began to lead her through the exercise. "Easy."

"Done?" Rose asked after a few minutes.

"Are you kidding? We just started. We'll do the isometrics and then you're free. Press your foot against my palm. Now relax. Again."

Annie counted backward from twenty.

"Done, yet?"

"Good grief, have you always been addicted to soap operas?"

"Some days they're my thread to sanity," Rose admitted. "Gets lonely out here in the winter. No gardening, no sunshine."

"Oh, well, I never thought about that. Switch legs."

"I'm switching. I'm switching."

"Push. Relax. Push. Relax." They completed the set. "Okay, now we're done. Let me help you get your socks and shoes on. That reminds me. We need to get you Velcro sneakers."

"Great. Velcro sneakers and surgical hose. I'll start a fashion trend."

Holding out her arm, Annie stood with her knees braced as Rose carefully pulled herself up to hold the walker.

"How long will I need this?"

"Until we're walking laps at the Y without it."

Rose grumbled. "Well, that's just plain wrong."

"Rose?"

Rose looked down at Annie, who sat on the floor slipping on Rose's socks and shoes. "Yes?"

"I need to ask you a question."

"You've got three minutes."

Annie chuckled. "Just one question."

"Shoot."

"What did Will's father have?"

"Have?"

"What did he die from?"

Closing her eyes for a moment, as though hiding some secret pain from Annie, Rose sighed. "In the end it was pneumonia."

"In the end?" Annie said the words softly.

"Annie, he had a disease. I can't tell you any more than that."

"Oh, I'm sorry. You're right. I'm keeping you from your show." She stood.

"No," Rose grumbled. "That's not what I mean. It's Will. He doesn't want me to discuss his father. I promised."

"I don't understand. Can't you discuss it with me?"

Rose's face reflected her increasing discomfort with the topic. "Ask Will."

"I can't ask Will."

"Sure you can."

"Last night was the first time in all these years he has even suggested there was something else going on with his father. He shared a little, but the 'do not enter' signs were up all over. I couldn't betray our trust with a bunch of nosy questions."

"That's our Will," Rose said with a sigh. "'Do not enter' is right."

"What should I do?" Annie asked.

"Short of breaking his arm, I imagine you're just going to have to wait until he's good and ready."

"That's what I was afraid of."

"Let's just pray he doesn't wait until it's too late like his daddy."

Chapter Nine

So that was what women called a simple black dress.

Yeah, it was black.

Simple?

Anything but.

One simple black dress had transformed Annie Harris into a stunning mystery. Her dark hair was pulled back with a sparkly clip. She wore no jewelry except the pearl earrings he had given her.

The more Will observed, the more he realized there was something else different, something he couldn't define. A confidence, an aura.

Annie was a woman. A drop-dead gorgeous woman.

This new Annie left him confused and off-kilter. He didn't like feeling like a schoolboy vying for a girl's attention.

Will considered the issue as he watched her from across the room. Unobtrusively, of course. The idea was to keep an eye on Annie without looking as if he was keeping an eye on Annie. Big brother, best buddy–like, he assured himself.

Seemed he wasn't the only one with that idea. In fact, judging by the attention she had garnered so far this evening, there were quite a few people interested in the sleek mystery woman in black, and they were mostly guys.

Will glanced around at the ample turnout for the Sullivan Ranch–KidCare launch party Margaret had thrown. Annie was as much a part of Sullivan Ranch and the success they'd enjoyed so far as he was. Yet he'd hardly even caught her eye since they'd arrived.

Fact was, since the small country western band had started playing an hour ago, she'd fended off more cowboys than any other woman in the room.

Will had also seen the frequent sweep of Annie's hand gesturing toward her healing leg, and the refusals to dance.

His ears perked as the band gathered back on the small stage for the next set. This time they struck up the notes of a popular song. He recognized the "missing my girl, got a horse for a best friend" tune. Noting Annie was alone, he decided maybe if he was quick enough, he could get across the room to keep her company.

See if she needed moral support. After all, this was her first social outing, and because it was understood that was what friends did. Help each other when needed, so to speak.

Too late.

Some yahoo had her cornered and was no doubt telling her tall tales.

Will's stomach clenched.

He must be hungry. The dessert table overflowed with delicacies. No expense had been spared for this spread. Surely something would satisfy him.

After filling a small china plate with a variety of sweets, he stood against the wall and hummed to the music, tapping the toe of his new black boots and watching the activity. From across the room Ed Reilly caught his eye. The older man gave him a nod of acknowledgment.

Will popped another pastry into his mouth. By the time the song was over the dish in his hand was empty. He frowned and examined the crumbs, wondering what he'd eaten.

The band played the introductory chords to a second number, a slow piece, this one a sweet, sentimental, old gospel ballad. Will set down his plate, and again prepared to cross the room to catch Annie. A feminine hand on his arm stopped him.

"Hey, Will," Joanie LaFarge smiled. "Official congratulations on your new venture."

"Thanks, Joanie."

"This sure is nice of the Reillys."

Will nodded in agreement. "Having a good time?"

"Are you kidding? Chris and I never get out. I would have been thrilled with pizza and a movie. But this…" She gestured around the room. "This is incredible. I guess Sullivan Ranch is in the big leagues now."

"Not hardly," Will said with a chuckle.

"Well, you better not tell Margaret that," Joanie said. "She's got you fast-tracking from rancher to Sullivan Ranch CEO. And she's talking you up like you're on a political ticket."

"No worries. I'm sure you and Chris will keep me grounded."

Joanie laughed. "Yes. Chris will have you mucking those stables with him if your head gets bigger than your ego."

"Yeah, he will."

"Are you talking about me again, Sullivan?"

Will greeted Chris with a handshake.

"Where's your girl?" Chris asked.

"My girl?"

"Annie." Chris looked around, his gaze finding Annie and Ryan the same time Will's did. "Aww, who introduced her to Doc Jones? Now that was a mistake."

"Margaret's been matchmaking," Will said.

"There's nothing wrong with a little shove in the right direction," Joanie offered. "But clearly Annie is not the match for Ryan."

"Thank you, Joanie," Will said. "That's exactly what I told Margaret."

"No, he's not the cowboy Annie has her eye on," she said, with a wink to her husband.

"What?" Will looked over his shoulder and spotted Annie, Jones at her side grinning like a fool.

Chris took a long sip of his tea and shook his head. "Oh, boy, Sullivan. You really don't get it, do you?"

"I'm missing something here, aren't I?"

Joanie patted his arm. "It's okay. Men are always slower than women when it comes to these things. Ask Chris."

Will glanced around for his beverage glass, the conversation suddenly making him awful thirsty. "Every time I set something down it disappears."

Chris laughed. "The bar's over there."

"Thanks," Will said.

A moment later, he discovered himself elbow to elbow with Ryan Jones.

"Club soda and lime," Will told the bartender.

"Sullivan." Ryan nodded a greeting, placing his order for two colas.

"Hey, Doc. Haven't seen you in a while. I must be doing something right."

Ryan smiled. "Probably not. Find an equine vet yet?"

"Yeah. Got a new guy lined up."

"You better. That horse of yours needs someone familiar before she delivers."

"You're familiar with her."

"Only by default. You should have gotten a new vet when yours retired."

"I did, if you recall. Twice. One had twins and the other moved."

"Sad story. Well, I've got enough to do with my

practice. I don't even have time to get out and see my own horse."

"That's a shame, Doc."

"Yeah. I can see you're heartbroken. Which reminds me— where have you've been hiding Annie all this time?"

"She's only been home two weeks."

"Why didn't I meet her years ago?"

"I don't know. You tell me. As I recall you only had eyes for Kait Field. By the way, whatever happened with you two?"

"Okay, okay," Ryan interrupted, one palm raised in gesture. "Let's not go there."

"And for the record," Will said, "I have not been hiding Annie."

Ryan raised his brows. "A mite touchy, aren't you?"

"Just concerned. She's been through a traumatic event."

"I know. She told me."

"She talked to you about her mission trip?"

"Yeah."

"You two sure have done an awful lot of talking, haven't you?"

"We've talked some."

"Well, don't let her overdo herself tonight."

"Don't worry. I intend to take good care of Annie. She's a very special woman."

"She's a good kid," Will agreed tightly.

There was a silence as Will received his drink from the bartender. Why did he suspect there was something else on Jones's mind? He glanced at the other man.

"What?"

"Mind if I drive her home tonight?"

"Who?" Will asked.

"Annie, Will. Annie."

"The ranch is a good five, six miles out of your way." Will stated the obvious.

"I don't remember you being this dense in high school," Ryan said, scratching his head.

Will glared. "So you're asking my permission?" Raising the glass in his hand, he took a long a swig, his mouth suddenly dry as dust. He didn't like the direction this conversation was taking. *Didn't like it at all.*

Ryan raised his brows. "Wanted to show due respect to her elders."

Elders?

Will nearly spewed his drink.

Will poured himself another tall one, though he supposed sitting in the dark kitchen drinking wasn't going to solve anything. One hand was wrapped around the chilled milk glass, while the other absently played with a note, moving the paper in and out between his fingers.

A telephone message he'd taken earlier. Nothing would satisfy him more than to crumple the little scrap and toss it in the trash. But there were only so many times he could tell the man to call back next week. Besides, he'd been raised to do the honorable thing. Which was no less than stinking irritating at times.

Like right now.

Besides, this time the man from medical missions had let some interesting information slip. Information Will intended to get to the bottom of.

Will glanced at the luminous dials of his watch. The party had been over for two hours.

Where was Annie?

Annie is a woman, not a child. He repeated the words silently. *She'll be home anytime now.* His mind raced with a running commentary.

She was with Ryan Jones. The man had volunteered to be in a bachelor auction. What did that say about his character?

And for that matter, what did he really know about the guy? Back in high school he'd been an honor student and on the basketball team. He'd gone to college in state and then vet school. Now he had a practice in Granby, catering mostly to small animals. Not an equine specialist, he came out to Sullivan Ranch more as a courtesy to Will as anything else. He also boarded a horse at the ranch. A horse he seldom had time to ride due to his busy schedule.

Will always thought Jones was a straight shooter, but that was Annie he was standing so close to. The current situation threw a whole new light on things.

Then again, it had occurred to Will that the situation might be a good thing. If Annie dated Jones, she'd have a reason to stay. Maybe he could talk some sense into her.

Will shook his head and took another swig.

No, that plan didn't sit well with him, either. If he was going to have to get used to the idea of Annie being with someone he sure didn't want it to be in plain sight. That could prove to be more painful than he wanted to consider.

A moment later he heard the crunch of tires on gravel through the open kitchen windows. A car door shut.

Should he hit the stairs running before she got her key in the door, or stay here in the dark and hope she'd pass right by and not notice him waiting up?

He chose the latter.

The way his luck was running it seemed no surprise when the kitchen light came on, blinding him.

"Did you drink *all* the milk?" Annie asked, as she tossed a beaded black clutch on the table and yanked open the refrigerator door.

"Hi to you, too."

She turned slightly and narrowed her eyes but said nothing.

"'Course I didn't drink it all. There's a little left."

"Define 'a little.'" Pulling a clean glass from the dishwasher, she poured the remaining milk and tossed the carton into the recycle bin. "Any cookies left?"

"Somebody cranky?"

Hands on hips she stared him down. "My feet hurt. My leg aches. My head is throbbing and I'm starving."

Will bit his tongue to keep from reminding her that if she hadn't been the center of attention all night she might have had a minute to eat and rest her feet. "So take off your shoes." He got up and grabbed the entire cookie jar, setting the brown ceramic pot on the table.

"Have you ever noticed you never do anything halfway?" She kicked her shoes under the table and slid into a chair.

"Nope."

"Nope, you never do anything halfway or nope, you never noticed?"

"Both."

She reached into the jar and pulled out three cookies. "Thank goodness. I've been thinking about these cookies for hours."

"Have fun tonight?" he asked. Her smoky eye makeup was slightly smudged and her lipstick had faded. Yet she was more alluring now than any woman at the party tonight.

"I suppose," she finally answered. "But being social is exhausting. Let's not do that again real soon, okay?" She broke a cookie in half and nibbled.

"All right with me, but Jones may have other ideas."

"Ryan's a good guy."

"So they keep telling me." He reached across the table to swipe the other half of Annie's cookie.

"Hey," she groused. "I bet you've already had six."

"If we run out I'll make more."

"And I'll rewire the Jeep," she muttered.

"What did you say?"

"You heard me."

"I'm going to have to tell Rose on you."

Unfazed by his threat, she didn't break a smile. "You do that, cowboy."

Will narrowed his eyes and leaned closer. "Who are you and what have you done with Annie?" he asked, folding the little note in his hand into a minuscule square.

"I can't be Little Annie Sunshine all the time."

"I guess not. But some sort of warning might be nice. We could clear the area of animals and small children."

This time she did smile.

"So, looks like you and Jones hit it off."

"Like minds," she said, thoughtfully examining the cookie.

"Now there is a scary thought."

"How many chocolate chips do you suppose there are in one cookie?"

"You're a strange woman," Will said. "I guess that's why you two had so much to talk about."

"Actually we were discussing matters of the heart. Ryan is a wounded soul."

Will released a guffaw. "Wounded, my saddle." He straightened in his seat. "That's the sort of thing a guy says to a woman to make her feel sorry for him."

"Oh. A pickup line? I suppose we dumb females fall for it every time. Is that what you're saying?"

Will opened his mouth and immediately closed it. A wise man knows when to back out carefully when he discovers he's stepped into a large cow patty. "That's not what I meant."

"Are you saying he's full of manure?"

"No. I'm saying I know guys."

"And I don't?"

"I sure hope not."

"Hmm. I'm not sure if that's a compliment or an insult."

"So," he said, trying to move things along, "you discussed Jones and his broken engagement."

"No. He didn't mention an engagement. What engagement?"

"Maybe you should ask him."

"Couldn't you just tell me, Will?"

"Don't know if that would be right."

Annie snorted. A girly snort, but a snort nonetheless. "Please. You know you are dying to tell me."

"Guys don't gossip."

She snorted again. "Uh-huh. Good one."

"So what exactly *were* you two talking about?"

"Philosophical things. Heartache. Unrequited love."

"You were dispensing advice on heartache and unrequited love?"

"I said we were talking."

"What makes you an expert on the subject?"

"I never claimed to be an expert," she said, her

voice taut and edgy. Her hands were clenched on the table.

Will realized she was getting mad. Plain mad. His brain scrambled backward to figure out what he'd said.

Too late.

She stood and half stomped, half limped to the sink with her empty glass. "You apparently have this image of me as some sort of kid. I'm not a child, Will, I'm a—well, *I am not a child.*"

Will averted his eyes from her perfectly silhouetted form standing against the sink in the black dress. A shudder went through him. A man could only handle so much.

No, she sure was not a child. Hoo boy. He'd grant her that.

"Hey, look. I'm teasing you," he said softly. "It just comes natural, like breathing. I didn't mean to hurt your feelings. You're right. It is an eye-opener to consider Miss Anne E. has had her heart broken."

She whirled around. "Why? Why should you be surprised? I'm not like my mother. I don't fall in love at the flip of a Stetson."

"Ouch. Annie, I never said that."

The silence in the room became tense. He could hear her breathing as he stared down at the table. "So who is this fella who broke your heart?"

"Once again you are misinterpreting what I am saying. I did not say my heart was broken. I simply empathize with what it is like to care for someone who doesn't reciprocate your feelings." She sat back down at the table and toyed with the few crumbs in front of her.

"Skirting round the question?"

She sighed in response.

"If you won't tell me who it is, how can I break his nose for you?"

"I'm being serious, Will."

"So am I," he said, creasing the paper in his hand.

"What *is* that you keep playing with?" Annoyance laced her voice as she snatched the note from his fingers.

"Phone message."

"For me?" She unfolded the paper. "I can barely read this. Do you think you wrinkled it enough?"

"It's from that medical missions program."

"Yes, I can see that."

"They sure call awfully late."

"For goodness' sake, they're in another time zone." She pointed to the faded numbers scrawled on the paper. "Is that a two?"

"I guess. You're not thinking of going again, are you?"

"I'm too tired to think, period."

"Annie, you're sidestepping me. The guy who called last week mentioned Mexico."

"You never told me they called last week."

"You never said anything about Mexico."

"Don't change the subject, Will."

"Okay, I'm sorry. I sort of forgot. His name was

Martin or…" Will tapped his fingers on the table trying to remember the guy's name.

"Morrow?"

"Yeah. That's him. He mentioned your paperwork for Mexico had been mailed."

"Mexico had been planned long before my…before the accident."

"You were going from Africa straight to Mexico?"

"They were tentative plans."

"And now?"

She stared at him, bold and unapologetic. "What do you want me to say, Will?"

"You *can't* be thinking of leaving so soon. Your leg—"

"My leg is fine. Rose's doctor looked at it Thursday. And I have an appointment coming up with my doctor in a week."

"What about Rose's therapy?"

"She's progressing well ahead of schedule."

"Doesn't make much sense to me. Your trunk just arrived Friday and now you're going to send it right back?"

She didn't answer, her dark eyes focused somewhere besides here and now.

"Hey." Will snapped his fingers in front of her face. "Are you listening to me?"

"I am," she answered, her gaze meeting his again.

"Are you going to answer the question?" he persisted, suddenly annoyed.

"What exactly is the question, Will?"

"Annie," he said softly, "are you leaving?"

"I don't know."

"When they call back, what will you say?"

"How can I answer that honestly?" Her hands opened and closed in obvious frustration.

Without thinking, he reached out and stopped the agitated movement. His large hand held her small one, and it fit perfectly. He stared into her dark eyes, lost for a moment. "I can give you a million reasons why you should stay."

She exhaled the breath, and Will caught a glimpse of sadness in her eyes before she shook her head and stared down at the paper.

Had he imagined her whispered words?

"Yes, but not the right one."

Chapter Ten

"**W**ill, there's a delivery truck blocking the driveway. Ellen can't get out," Rose called into the house through the screen door.

"Be right there." He left the table, lunch uneaten, and grabbed a ball cap before heading out the door.

"What about your sandwich?" Annie said.

His cell phone ringing prevented a response. "Sullivan Ranch." The screen slammed shut behind him as he jogged down the drive. "I don't have a calendar in front of me. Could I call you back in about ten minutes? Sure. Thanks."

With any luck the delivery was the refrigerator and freezer he'd ordered for the barn, which was supposed to have arrived yesterday.

"Sorry, Ellen," he said, as he passed Rose's sister in her ancient tan Buick.

The white truck at the end of the drive had Wilson Wholesale Meats in large letters on the side. Will gritted his teeth. The meat was early, the freezer was late.

"I've got fifty pounds of frankfurters for Sullivan," the driver called with a wave of his clipboard.

"I'm Sullivan. I need the boxes delivered to the front door."

"Can't get up the driveway, and I sure ain't rolling my dolly all the way up there over that pea gravel."

"Let the Buick out and you can get in."

"Will," Annie called from the house, "Ed Reilly is on the phone."

"Have him call my cell, please."

"I told him that already, but apparently he still can't get through."

Will stopped at Ellen's car. "Okay. He's backing out for you."

"Thank you, Will. Say, when is that secondary driveway going to be done?"

Will glanced at the sky. "We were rained out yesterday. Weather permitting, they're going to attempt to pour concrete again tomorrow."

"There's a relief. Another brilliant Annie idea, wasn't that?"

"Sure was."

"You best not let that gal go. Sullivan Ranch needs her."

"You're right, Ellen." He gave the hood of the Buick a friendly thump before he went back to the house.

Rose sat on the porch with her walker and watched as he took the steps two at a time. She looked up from her crocheting. "Chris stopped by. Said that new vet called. He's coming out tomorrow. Chris will be with him, to show him around the stable and introduce him to Okie."

"Thanks, Rose."

"Oh, and Pastor Jameson wants to know why you aren't signed up for the men's breakfast next month."

"I don't think I've got breakfast or lunch penciled in for the rest of this year."

"Will."

"Kidding, Rose. I'll call him—later. Much later."

In the kitchen he caught Annie. "Can you do me a couple of favors?"

"You mean a couple more, right?" She grinned. "Sure, boss."

"Funny."

She reached for a pencil and notebook from the table, a comically eager expression on her face. Will paused for a moment and chuckled. "I'm glad you can see the humor in this."

"Ease up, boss. Everything will work out. One way or another. Now what can I do to help?"

"Could you put the meat in the fridge when they get to the door? Please. And could you make a few calls? Track down the freezer and refrigerator." He pulled a yellow receipt out of his wallet and handed it to her.

"I can handle that. What else, boss?"

Will narrowed his eyes. She was enjoying this way too much. "I've got a few reservations that need to be confirmed. Everything is in that black binder on my desk, highlighted in yellow. All you have to do is call the contact person and review the information. Jot down who you spoke with and the date and time in the notebook."

"Okay, sounds easy enough."

"Thanks. Maybe I do need to put you on the payroll."

"Let's not go overboard. I think a few trips to the mall should be plenty of compensation."

"Deal. Let me take care of Ed and I'll be right back."

"Sure."

Will strode into his office and picked up the headset and depressed the speakerphone button. "Ed, sorry to keep you waiting."

"Will, how are you?"

"Busy, real busy." Will grabbed a stack of unopened mail and began to slice open the envelopes.

"So my wife tells me. Sure you haven't bitten off more than you can chew?"

"Busy is a good thing, Ed."

Ed chuckled. "Did a follow-up on your first two programs and we have satisfied customers. They'll be calling us again in the fall."

"Glad to hear that."

"So tell me more about the catering."

"I used the catering company Margaret suggested for the first projects but I'm doing things myself for the smaller programs."

"How are you managing that?"

"Remodeling the old barn. Have freezers and a refrigerator on order. Working on permits now."

"The thing is, Will, I like to support my vendors. They in turn support KidCare."

"I understand that, Ed. But my contract with KidCare doesn't specify which vendors I utilize. I take your recommendations out of respect for your knowledge of this business. You're the pro. I'm the new guy. But when I can come up with a better idea, I have to give it a shot."

Annie appeared at the door of the office, a pained expression on her face.

"Ed, I really have to go."

"We can finish this later," Ed agreed. "Can you stop by the house tomorrow evening?"

Will leaned back in his chair. *Just what he needed. Another meeting.* "Sure, Ed. I'll see you then."

Will pressed the disconnect button and tossed the letters in his hand on the growing pile. He looked at Annie.

"Where am I going to put all that meat?" she asked.

"Is that a trick question?"

"Will, there isn't room."

"Any luck tracking down the refrigerator and freezer?"

"The manager says his men got lost yesterday. He promised delivery by the end of the day."

"Call the Dearbornes. They've got a huge freezer they use for venison. See if they can help us out for a few hours. I'll have Chris run it over."

Annie left the room, shaking her head and muttering.

Will sat back down in his chair and ran a hand over his jaw. There were bills to be paid, the business checkbook to balance, receipts and invoices to log in. Reservation requests to respond to. Even the web page was becoming a nemesis, with dozens of email queries in his in-box.

His to-do list was becoming endless. He was seriously drowning in details. Going under fast without a life jacket.

His body began to shake and a cold chill passed over him.

"Something is not right," he whispered, as once again his hands trembled.

Reaching over to his desk drawer he pulled out his wallet and removed a faded white business card: Dr. Thomas Nolan—Neurologist.

"Blood pressure's a little high, but you always get white-coat syndrome as I recall." Dr. Nolan glanced from Will to the chart in his hands.

"I'm having symptoms of the disease." The words tumbled from Will's mouth. Just saying them provided a measure of relief.

"Tell me about it."

"Tremors, irritability, memory problems. And insomnia. I don't think I've had a full night's sleep in weeks." Will looked around the neurologist's office, taking in first the certificates on the wall, then pictures of a doting family on a bookshelf. *A wife and three children.*

"Son, generally I'd say you're too young for symptoms. Your father didn't have early onset, so I doubt if you will."

"And that means?"

"It means if you have the disease I don't expect to see indications at earliest until you are in your late thirties, early forties."

"So I have another ten years before my life is over?"

Dr. Nolan cleared his throat. "There are medications for the chorea symptoms, when and if you need them."

"Yeah, that's what I hear. Drugs for the tics. Drugs for the depression. Drugs for the memory. Plenty of drugs. I'm starting to understand my father a little better." Will fiddled with his hat resting on his lap. His gaze met the physician's. "So why am I having the shakes?"

"You blood work indicates low blood sugar. Are you on any medications that I'm not aware of?"

"No."

"Do you eat three balanced meals?"

Will shrugged. He wished his life was that simple. "When I remember."

"Start remembering. You're going to have to monitor your intake. Smaller meals more frequently to keep those levels stable. Keep a juice box at your bedside for when you wake up. A lot of people have low blood sugar. It's easily regulated. Keep yourself hydrated. Drink plenty of water while you're working at the ranch, especially now that hot weather is on the way."

Will nodded.

"I'm sending you down the hall for a session with a dietician. Takes about an hour. She happened to have a cancellation, so this is your lucky day."

"Think so?"

"Yes. She'll give you a little snack so you don't pass out on your way home."

"Thanks. But what about the insomnia?"

"Have you been under more stress than usual lately?"

"Yeah, you could say that." Will laughed. "Doing my best to save the ranch."

"That's enough to keep anyone awake at night. Hard to stop the cycle once it starts."

Will shot him a questioning glance.

"Lack of sleep is followed by irritability, then more lack of sleep, and more irritability." The doctor paused. "Drinking more coffee and soda than usual?"

"All of the above."

"That will contribute to the cycle. Stick to water."

Will nodded again.

"You want a script for a mild sleeping pill?"

"No. No." *No drugs. He was adamant about that.* "Let me try to get a handle on things on my own first."

"Fair enough." Dr. Nolan leaned forward. "By the way, keeping secrets is another stressor."

"What are you talking about? Secrets?"

"Who have you shared this with?"

"What do you mean?"

"The Huntington's."

"Are you kidding? No one but Rose."

"You have every right not to be tested. But it's still in your best interest to develop a support system. A pastor or a counselor. Friends and family members." He opened the lower drawer of his desk. "Here's a list of family counselors in the area."

Will took the pamphlet and turned it over. "I'll give it some thought."

"You're going to have to do more than think about it. To tell you the truth, Will, I'm more concerned with your overall health than Huntington's. You're showing all the signs of physical and emotional breakdown. Every symptom you mentioned can be attributed to stress. Even the low blood sugar. You're stressed and forgetting to eat. Bottling every thing inside is giving you insomnia. Stress can kill you."

"So can Huntington's."

"I think you better focus on today and quit worrying about tomorrow. I want to see you back in here in a month for another checkup. I'll expect some lifestyle changes."

"You're sure it's stress?"

"Son, I don't get paid to lie to you. Do yourself a favor and get a counselor. You can't hold everything inside and can't do it all yourself. Your father had the same type A personality. It didn't help him and it isn't helping you. I like to think you learned something from your father's mistakes."

Will opened and closed the brochure. He released a deep breath.

"I know this isn't what you want to hear. Maybe part of you wants to hear it is the Huntington's. An easy answer. But that door hasn't opened yet."

He stared at Will long and hard. "What you're experiencing now you are doing to yourself. Take a day off. Relax. Have some fun. Forget about the Huntington's for a few hours every week."

"Easier said than done."

"Maybe so. But whether you take my advice or continue to do what you've always done is completely up to you, Will. So are the consequences."

"Will."

Will stiffed. Rolling down his shirtsleeve, he forced himself to relax before he turned at the sound of Annie's voice in the clinic hallway.

Annie's and *Ryan's.*

Her face lit up as she approached him, and Will couldn't help but notice how lovely she looked, her dark hair long and free, a contrast to the yellow blouse she wore. New clothes from their shopping trip, he recalled. Yeah, Annie was a sunny picture all right, except for the tall shadow at her side.

"What are you two doing here?"

"Ryan brought me in for my checkup."

"I was supposed to do that, wasn't I?" Will asked,

with a disgusted shake of his head. *Dropped the ball again.* "You should have called me."

"I tried but your cell phone was off."

He pulled the phone off his belt. "Just can't get used to having to be available twenty-four-seven. Sorry. I turned it off when I went in for my exam." He nodded to Ryan. "Thanks for taking her."

"My pleasure." Ryan grinned, his expression amused.

You're enjoying this, aren't you, Jones? And don't I feel like a horse's behind?

"Are you sick?" Annie's question interrupted his thoughts. She looked him up and down with a furrowed brow of concern.

"Me? Naw. Annual physical and lab work."

"Old geezers have to check their cholesterol once a year, right, Sullivan?"

"You tell me, Doc." Will ran a hand over his face. "Don't know why I didn't think about your appointment when I was here, though. Lots on my mind lately. Sorry."

"Will, quit apologizing. It's really all right."

"You on your way in or out?" Will asked.

"I'm done," Annie said.

"What did the doctor say?"

"He wants me back in three weeks and then he'll okay me to go back to work."

"You sure you heard him right? That seems awfully soon to me."

"*Will.*"

"Hey, I'm glad you're mending without any problems, but it's only been how long since—"

"Five weeks."

"Who is this doctor? Did you check his credentials?"

"Will."

"How's Okie doing?" Ryan interjected.

"Coming along. She told me to tell you your horse misses you."

Ryan laughed and crossed his arms. "Funny, Sullivan. Did she mention her new vet?"

"Yeah. Said he wasn't nearly as goofy-looking as you."

"Did he mention the due date?" Ryan asked.

"Still right around the Fourth of July."

Ryan nodded. "This your first delivery?"

"Yeah. Last one was when my grandfather was alive." Will smiled at the thought. Lots of firsts since he'd taken over the ranch.

Annie glanced up at Ryan, then back at him. "We're going to a movie and late lunch. Do you want to join us?"

Will, too, glanced at the other man. Oh, yeah, Jones would love him to join them. That much was evident. A nice little threesome.

"Southern Hills?" Will asked.

"That work for you?" Ryan's lips twitched, enjoying the exchange.

Will turned to Annie. "Thanks for the invite, but I've got to get back to the ranch."

* * *

Will rapped on the door of the old Tudor estate. Hands in his pockets, he turned to admire the other houses along the old moneyed neighborhood of Utica Square.

Margaret Reilly greeted him with a smile and led him down the hall and into a small parlor.

"Coffee?" she asked.

"No, thanks, I'm cutting back. Water would be great."

He sat and glanced around the sitting room. The air smelled like candle wax and oranges. For some reason he couldn't shake the feeling he had just been scheduled for a surprise visit to the dentist. Somehow he knew this was going to be one of those painful but necessary appointments.

A moment later, Ed Reilly strode into the room, with Margaret at his side.

"Ed." Will rose.

"Will. Hey, glad you could make it."

Margaret handed Will a glass of water and he took a deep swallow.

Why did he feel that uneasiness in the pit of his gut? He set down his glass on a crystal coaster and shoved his restless hands back into his pants pockets.

"Sit, Will, sit. This won't take long. I just wanted to review where we're going."

Will nodded.

"Let me say that I have been very pleased with

our relationship with you and Sullivan Ranch. The numbers are positive. Our clients are happy. All of that makes us both look good. But now that the renovation is complete and projects are moving forward, we want you to start thinking long-term. Margaret and I feel a certain responsibility for you and Sullivan Ranch."

"Responsibility?" He couldn't help sound confused.

Ed leaned back in a leather wing chair and gestured with his hands. "Perhaps that isn't the correct term. Let me explain. We're grooming you for, well, for big things. You have that much potential, Will." With a grin, Ed turned and smiled at his wife.

"Thanks, Ed. But as I've told Margaret, I'm not sure that's where I want to go."

"Don't rule it out. You and Sullivan Ranch must continue to grow and that means extending your reach."

"You have to run in the right circles, maintain certain decorum," Margaret interjected. "Get a little more involved, socially." She paused. *"With the right people."*

"Expand your network to extend your reach," Ed said with a satisfied nod.

The words sounded like an advertising campaign. Will swallowed hard as Ed repeated the pitch yet again.

"Don't think I don't know it isn't easy, Will. I'm a loner just like you. But sometimes you have to do what's necessary to grow the business. These are difficult times, son. Business doesn't just walk up to your door. While you have KidCare marketing supporting you, it's important that you do your part."

"Okay. Well, I see where you're coming from, Ed. But what exactly is it you want me to do right now? Because I have to tell you, I'm running on empty ninety percent of the time. I flat-out do not have any more energy to give anyone."

"All I want you to do is to start thinking about *extending your reach.* Sullivan Ranch can't grow unless you do."

Will's cell phone began to ring, and he grabbed it off his belt. "Sullivan," he answered. "Yeah, Chris. Great. Thanks for the update. I'll be home real soon."

Margaret lifted a brow. "Is everything all right?"

"The vet stopped by to check on Okie. She's almost ready to drop foal. Everything is looking good."

Ed nodded.

"I probably should get going. I want to talk to Chris before he leaves for the night."

"One more thing before you go. Will, Margaret's been feeling some resistance from you, and I want you to work on relaxing. She's been working with KidCare for a long time. Give her a chance. Can you do that?"

Will released a breath. "Okay, sure."

"Give some of her ideas a try before you jump straight to no."

"I'll work on that."

"Thanks." Ed stood, gripped his hand and gave him a slap on the back. "We think a lot of you, Will, and we know you won't let us down."

Will nodded, eager to get back to the ranch.

Chapter Eleven

"I thought you liked Doc Jones," Annie said, as she dumped the softened shortening into a large bowl.

"Don't *dislike* him," Rose replied, turning the page of the Granby newspaper and then smoothing it flat on the kitchen table. "All I said was that he sure has been hanging around here more than usual lately."

"Twice, besides taking me for my checkup. Both times he said he was checking on Okie as a favor to Will."

"Checking on you is more like the truth. Will has a fancy horse vet for Okie now."

Annie shrugged. "Ryan's lonely. He's happy for conversation and a glass of lemonade."

"Tell that to Will."

"Why should it bother Will? In fact he was fortunate Ryan was here last week when that girl was tossed. She hurt herself and the horse."

Rose merely made a "harrumph" under her breath.

"Maybe I should put pecans in this batch," Annie

commented. "It might dissuade Will from eating them so fast."

"Will? Ryan has had a good share, too. If Will finds out he's got competition for your oatmeal cookies he's going to grouse loud and long, and you can count on that."

Annie cracked an egg and disposed of the shell. "What is it about Ryan that bothers you?" she persisted, determined to get to the bottom of Rose's attitude.

"I don't begrudge Ryan the conversation and lemonade. Just want you to keep in mind that he's a man on the rebound."

"His engagement was over almost ten years ago."

"Not in his heart."

"What does that mean?" Annie chuckled and tried to find a grain of logic in the statement.

"It means he'll be thinking of another woman all the time he's courting you."

"Courting? Who said anything about courting?" She waved the spatula in confusion.

"Don't have to say the words out loud for them to be true."

"Rose, really. We're just friends. Nothing more."

"Annie, you're the first woman who has had his interest in all these years. Just don't forget that Ryan's heart is still promised to another woman."

Had Rose heard a word she'd said? Ryan was simply a friend. Annie paused and stared down at the floor. "Tell me about this other woman."

"Kait Field. You look a lot like her, except she had that exotic look of Cherokee heritage. Those high cheekbones. And her hair was black like Will's not chocolate brown like yours. She and Ryan were sweethearts all through high school and college. She took off the night of college graduation."

"What happened?"

"Some think the high-and-mighty Jones family sent her on her way."

Annie stopped what she was doing to listen to Rose. *Poor Ryan. He really was a tortured soul.* She stirred the batter slowly as she contemplated the fate of the young lovers.

"Do you believe in true love, Rose?"

"True love? Not sure I understand that word. Sounds like the emphasis is on the romantic."

"Isn't love supposed to be romantic?" Annie asked.

"Love is a lot of things. You've read Corinthians. Doesn't get more plain than that."

"Love always hopes. Love never fails."

"That's a big challenge right there," Rose said.

"I never thought about it like that."

"You ought to. Romance is a wonderful thing, but when push comes to shove, love is just like faith. A step in the dark. A choice."

"You're right, Rose. How'd you get to be so smart?"

"I'm old as dirt. You don't get to be my age without a few hard lessons along the way."

"Have you ever been in love?" Annie asked.

Rose glanced at Annie, a beatific smile appearing on her face, transforming her countenance. "Oh, yes. Still am." She cleared her throat. "Enough about me. Now, what is it we were discussing?"

"Ryan and his broken heart."

"Pshaw. Don't you worry about Ryan. The Lord has a plan for him, too."

"Do you think so?"

"Of course. In the meantime you be careful not to encourage him." She scoffed. "That man is much too handsome for his own good. And those bedroom eyes."

"Bedroom eyes?" Annie's head jerked up. She laughed loudly this time. "Now how did I miss that? And for that matter, what are bedroom eyes? I mean, as opposed to kitchen eyes or bathroom eyes."

Rose removed her glasses and folded up the paper. "Men don't talk like women, Annie. You have to read their eyes. Now our Will, for example, has kitchen eyes."

"You can say that again."

"Say what again?" Will asked, tossing a straw cowboy hat on a chair.

The inviting grin he shot Annie sent tiny chills through her. She focused on stirring the batter.

Will leaned over and examined the bowl. "There's nuts in there," he complained.

"We said that if you eat any more cookies you were going to start looking like one," Annie said. She gently slapped his hand away.

Will patted his flat abdomen through the denim

shirt. "Six-pack abs. Comes from hard work, not some fancy gym."

"What a cowboy thing to say." She shook her head and spooned out dough.

"Do you have time to help me with that paperwork?" he asked.

"Sure. Soon as the cookies are done."

"You hire Annie as your secretary, Will?"

"More like all round gofer," Annie said.

"What can I say?" Will asked. "I interviewed three others but she was the only one who could do CPR and bake cookies while she filed invoices."

Rose laughed. "Oh, you're joshing me now."

"Annie tell you we won't be here for dinner?" he asked.

Rose nodded. "Singles supper and concert at the church. Yes, I heard."

"I'm still not sure I want to go," Annie said, as she opened the oven door.

Rose turned and her gaze connected with Annie's. "That's because you overdid yourself at Margaret's party. You haven't been out of the house hardly at all since then. Don't think I haven't noticed you know the names of all the characters in my soap opera."

This time it was Will who burst out with a hard laugh.

"Hey, I'm having lots of fun," Annie said. "Joanie has me exercising the horses. And I've helped cut the grass on the riding mower. Tomorrow Chris is going to let me do the entire thing by myself."

"That's your idea of fun?" Will asked with a shake

of his head. "Last time we discussed fun, I ended up at the mall. Now you're talking about a riding mower like it was a lap at Indy."

"I also went to Binding Stevens three times this week."

"Buying flowers doesn't count either," Rose said.

"But don't they look nice?" she asked. Rose gave her free reign with the color scheme for this year's perennials and ignored the fact that Annie had gone overboard filling every container she could get her hands on with soil and small plants. It had been so satisfying to pick out the flowers and plant them.

"The yard looks lovely, but you need to have some real fun," Rose said. "Soon enough you'll be back to work and wishing you'd taken more time to relax."

"Work?" Will asked, perking up. "Do you know something I don't know?" He glanced at both Rose and Annie.

"No, but I'm trying to be realistic. Annie isn't one to sit still, and the doctor told her he'd give her a release after eight weeks. That is coming up here soon."

"I can't believe I'm hearing this from you, Rose," Will said.

"I didn't say she could move out of the Tulsa area or anything."

"Still, that's a mighty mature attitude," Will said.

"Mature?" Rose laughed. "That's another word for *old,* isn't it? Which reminds me. Since you both are going to be out of the house, I thought I'd take the opportunity and have a few of the church ladies over. Ellen is coming by to help me get things ready."

"You won't be kicking up a row again, will you? Gets embarrassing when they call the sheriff," Will said, eyeing the cookies through the glass window of the oven.

"He's in rare form, isn't he?" Rose looked to Annie.

"I thought it was something you put in his oatmeal. He's been like this all week."

Rose glanced out the window. "There's the mail truck."

"I'll get the mail," Annie said.

Will followed right behind.

"Getting your exercise?" she asked, noting his strides matched hers down the drive.

"Walking pretty good these days, aren't you?" Will countered. She increased her pace, but he still kept up.

With a grin Annie began to jog away from him.

"Hey, I want to talk to you."

At the road she pulled open the mailbox and gathered the periodicals and envelopes. "The amount of junk mail you get is incredible."

"Yeah, I've noticed 'Resident' gets more mail than I do. Sure beats bills, so I'm not complaining."

"What did you want to talk about?" she asked, handing him a small package.

"Well, I was thinking maybe we should all go together."

"Together?"

"To the supper."

Annie nodded. "And which 'we' are you referring to?"

"Margaret asked me to escort a friend of hers. Joan or Jill? She's new in town and her father is negotiating a contract with KidCare. And I thought, well, since Ryan is picking you up and we're going to the same place, why not?"

"I really don't think that's a good idea."

He stared at her for a moment, before his eyes widened. "You want to spend time alone with Jones."

"No, that's not what I mean at all," she said, with a flash of irritation at his words. "I keep telling you we're only friends."

"Tell him."

"I don't need to tell Ryan. He and I communicate quite nicely."

"That right?" Will narrowed his eyes. "So if you two *communicate* so well, then what's the problem?"

The problem was it would pretty much kill her to be forced to sit around and watch as some friend of Margaret's fawned over Will. Not her idea of a good time.

"Annie?"

"*Fine,*" she huffed. "We can all go together. Whatever."

"You don't sound like it's fine," Will grumbled.

"Don't push your luck, Sullivan. I said it was fine." She leafed through the rest of the mail, handing things over to Will one at a time, but holding back a large envelope which she stuck under her arm.

"What do you have there?"

"This is probably the preliminary paperwork for my next trip."

"Mexico again."

"Maybe. But you knew it was coming."

"Yeah. And I also know you don't have to go. You do have a choice. Correct?" He said the last word slowly.

"Yes," she answered, knowing he was leading her somewhere she would probably regret going.

"Would you at least check out some of the hospitals here? Please?"

Annie released a breath. "Sure, Will. I'll do that."

"That was way too easy," he said, as they strolled back up the driveway.

"As it happens, I've already set up interviews at several hospitals. One of my good friends from nursing school is now a recruiter. We're meeting for lunch next week. I'm also preparing to send some résumés out."

"Why didn't you say so?"

"I guess because I'm trying to turn this over to God, not to Will."

He stopped short. "Is that how it seems?"

Her eyes met his but she didn't answer, not eager to offend him but unable to lie.

"I sound like a pretty heavy-handed guy." His voice reflected surprise at the observation.

"The word *stubborn* came to mind. Possibly even a little manipulative."

"Whoa. Wait a minute there. Stubborn I can maybe see. Sort of. Manipulative? How do you figure?"

"I spoke with the associate director of the medical missions program." She stopped and narrowed her eyes in challenge. "Apparently he's called on multiple occasions."

"I told you he called."

"Not numerous times."

Will rubbed a hand over his face and through his hair. "Busted." A dark curl dared to unfurl onto his forehead, and Annie barely resisted the urge to reach out and push it back in place.

She sighed but said nothing. When they reached the porch steps, Will turned to face her. "I'm sorry."

"Are you? Or would you do it again given the opportunity?"

He considered her words and shrugged. "Probably, but I'm still sorry. You know I'm just trying to protect Rose."

"Oh, Rose. So that's your story."

"Not going to forgive me?"

"Not going to let you off the hook."

Will groaned, his eyes tightly closed in mock pain.

"Look, Will, you're you and I'm me. You may be stubborn—"

"And manipulative," he added.

"And manipulative. But what was it you said I am? Impulsive? I think that was the word."

"I said that?"

"Maybe not verbatim, but you did say I tend to run through all the doors without stopping to see what God's plan for me is."

"My words sure get a lot of mileage, not to mention coming around to bite me in the backside," he mumbled.

Annie smiled. "Your words were a wake-up call. I said I was letting God in, but it was only on my terms. I kept such tight control on the situation there was no way I could have heard Him." She glanced over at Will and noted the confused expression on his face. "Uh-oh, now what are you thinking?"

"About what you just said."

Annie cocked her head. This time she was the one confused.

"You know, control and letting God in."

"I do know. It's my greatest downfall."

"Then we're a lot alike, you and I, Annie. Because I know I deal with the same thing on a daily basis."

"I supposed that's why we're such good friends, we're a lot alike and we can be honest with each other."

"Honest, huh? I think we're just two hardheads."

Annie laughed. "Maybe. But you should be flattered I'm taking your advice."

"*My* advice?"

"Sure. Because of your advice, I'm very conscious

to attempt to make this decision prayerfully, not with my head or my heart."

"I guess I ought to try taking my own advice."

She bit back a smile. "I'm not touching that."

This was by far one of his dumbest ideas yet. Will continued to peruse the dessert menu as the waitress took orders around the table.

He slid his chair a bit closer to Ryan and away from Jillian, but the woman seemed to have edged toward him yet again.

"You get any closer and people will start talking," Ryan muttered.

Will glared at him.

What was he thinking when he suggested going together? Avoiding one-on-one had been the original plan. Keep anyone from thinking this was a real date.

Instead the woman kept talking on and on as though they were an item. The whole thing was giving him a headache. Will was also pretty sure that his dentist would object to the amount of jaw-grinding he'd done so far tonight.

He glanced over at Ryan, who'd had a perpetual smile on his face since the moment they'd left the ranch. It was downright embarrassing how the guy hung on every word Annie said.

Will prided himself on his control and couldn't understand why he kept having an urge to slug the guy and wipe that smile off his face. Every time he looked over and saw Ryan's arm loped over the back of Annie's chair, his fingers brushing against her shoulder, Will twitched.

The waitress snapped her order book shut and stepped aside to allow the hostess and a parade of incoming patrons access to the back room of the popular eatery.

After dinner and the concert, the women had voted for dessert and coffee. If Will had his way, he'd have headed home hours ago.

At least they'd chosen one of the best pie places in the area. The restaurant and bakery was packed tonight, as usual. Will inhaled deeply, appreciating the aromas of fresh pastries.

"Glad you suggested this place, Annie. They serve the best pies in town," Ryan commented.

"Second-best," Will said. His words were echoed at the same exact moment by Annie. When his gaze connected with hers they laughed.

"What's the joke?" Jillian asked with a thin smile.

"Rose's pies are the best," Annie explained with a wink to Will.

He smiled back and looked beyond Annie to a familiar figure. Lulu Parson, with a man Will recognized as the retired Granby high school principal, Howard Reynolds, at her heels. Her fire-engine-red high heels.

Will couldn't help but notice that the years had not been as generous to Howard as they had been to his date.

Lulu stopped suddenly as her gaze met Will's. Howard nearly collided with her backside.

"Why, Will, how nice to see you again," Lulu smiled. "Taking your lovely wife out on the town I see."

Warmth crept up Will's neck, no doubt turning him the same shade of red as Lulu's lipstick. He didn't dare spare a glance around the table. "Good to see you, too, Ms. Parson."

"And Ryan Jones. How are you? Still as handsome as ever, I see."

"Hi, Ms. Parson. You're looking especially lovely tonight."

"Ryan, you never change." Lulu brushed a hand over her dress pleased at the compliment. She turned to the man at her side. "Howard, you remember Will Sullivan and Ryan Jones, don't you? I don't believe either of them spent any time in your office. They were such nice boys."

Annie's laughing eyes met Will's across the table; her expression told him she knew better.

"Aren't you going to introduce me to the young lady?" Lulu asked Ryan.

"Yes, ma'am," Ryan said. "This is Annie."

Lulu waved a white-gloved hand at Ryan. "I've already met Mrs. Sullivan. Howie, this is Annie. You remember I told you about her? She's the nurse."

A confused Ryan gave Will a look, begging his intervention. Dry-mouthed, Will picked up his water glass, only to be elbowed by Ryan midswig. Will gulped and nearly choked on his water, quickly setting the glass down. "Ms. Parson," Will said, "This is my friend Jillian."

Lulu offered Jillian a hand. "Pleased to meet you, Julie. You may call me Lulu."

Will cleared his throat. "It's uh, Jillian."

"Will's wife has enrolled in my yoga class at the Y. You're more than welcome to join us, Julie," Lulu continued without pause.

An amused Jillian took Lulu's proffered hand.

"Ms. Parson, would you and Mr. Reynolds care to join us?" Will asked. The courtesy smacked of disaster but was required etiquette nevertheless. "Maybe we could all move to a larger table."

"Oh, no, wouldn't dream of intruding. Besides, Howie and I want to be alone tonight. We're celebrating our engagement." In a loving gesture, she placed a hand on Howard Reynolds's arm.

"Engagement?" Annie spoke up. "That's wonderful. Congratulations."

Howard straightened and gazed adoringly at Lulu. He had a pronounced rhythmic tremor to his head and upper extremities.

"Yes, we were sweethearts when we were young, and drifted apart. But we were meant to be. Fifty years later and we still have that old spark," Lulu said proudly.

"I'm a l-l-lucky man," Howard stated, a heavy stutter evident, but overshadowed by the gleam in his eyes.

"Oh, that's so romantic, Ms. Parson," Annie said, her eyes dreamy as they focused on the couple.

"Isn't it?" Lulu agreed. "Fifty years is a long time to wait for true love. But Howard was worth the wait."

"Come along, Lulu, love, we'll leave these young people alone." Again the stutter was evident in Howard's speech.

"Congratulations, again," Will said, as the couple departed.

"Thank you. We'll send you all invitations to the wedding," Lulu said, as she left them.

"Oh, my goodness. What was wrong with that man?" Jillian asked Annie in a low voice.

Will's gut clenched at Jillian's repulsed tone.

"Parkinson's disease, I imagine," Annie replied quietly.

"How tragic to marry a man with a disease like that. Did you see how he shook, and his speech?"

"Tragic? For who? Lulu doesn't seem to notice anything but Howard's heart," Annie said with a thoughtful smile. "Isn't that what love is all about? What's inside. Not what's outside."

Jillian contemplated Annie's comment. "You're a nurse, so I suppose it's easier for you." She sipped her water and turned to Will. "Lulu seems to be a little confused. What was all that nonsense about Annie being your wife?"

"We're all out of lemon meringue," the waitress announced, a tray filled of desserts and a carafe of coffee in her arms.

Saved by the pie, Will realized.

Ryan leaned over to Will and spoke in a whisper,

"Speaking of pie. If I were a betting man, I'd bet you're in deep cow pie. Hope you're wearing your old boots."

Will glanced down at the floor with regret. "I seem to be a cow pie magnet these days."

Chapter Twelve

"You're awfully quiet," Ryan commented.

She turned from the railing to face him. His lanky form was draped on the porch swing, where he sat balancing a coffee mug on his knee. "More coffee?"

"I'm good, thanks."

"What are you thinking so hard about?" he asked.

"Mexico."

"Mexico. Now that's random."

Annie gave a short laugh. "I heard you went there on a mission trip."

"Oh, that was a few years back. Accompanied the youth group at church."

"How long was the trip?"

"Two weeks. The church bused the kids down there, and we spent most of the time teaching them carpentry skills, then building a church. The kids launched the first services and got to preach."

"Sounds like you enjoyed the time."

"Oh, yeah. Guess I forgot how much fun I had until you mentioned it. Probably should sign up to do it again real soon."

"Yes, it sounds like you should."

"Are you thinking about going to Mexico?" he asked.

"It is one of my options." She took a deep breath, wrapped her arms around the porch post and stared out at the trees silhouetted against the night sky in the distance. So many decisions to be made.

"More thinking?" he asked.

"Yes." She turned back again.

Ryan nodded thoughtfully. "What about?"

"Tonight."

"What *was* all that stuff with Ms. Parson?" he asked.

"Lulu is so deaf. She got it into her head I'm Will's wife, and that's all she wrote on that topic."

"That Lulu Parson is quite a character, isn't she?" he said, chuckling.

"Yes, and I hope I'm just like her when I'm a woman of mature years."

Ryan grinned at her words. "Yeah, I can see a little of Lulu in you already."

Annie met his gaze. "I'm beginning to see that maybe real love like Lulu and Howard have is a combination of both friendship and love."

Ryan fingered the edge of his Stetson and unfolded his long legs, setting his mug on the ground. He stood and ambled over to the railing. Taking her hands in his big ones, he faced her, the green eyes direct as they searched her face. "I'm banging my head against my saddle here, aren't I?" He smiled ever so sadly.

"I don't understand." She tilted her head and looked up at him, confused.

"I thought maybe you and I might have a chance." He stopped and shrugged.

"I'm so sorry," Annie said, gently pulling her hands from his. She quickly remembered Rose's warning in the kitchen. "I didn't mean to encourage you that way. I thought you understood." She took a deep breath as she assessed him. Ryan was a good guy, a real friend. A kind and Godly man, he would be easy to love. But she knew in her heart that there was a long line drawn in the dirt as far as their relationship was concerned.

"Don't be sorry," he said. "Totally my fault. You're right. I didn't understand. I do now."

She met his gaze with a question in her eyes.

"You're in love with Will," he said.

Annie's mouth seemed dry as a suitable response evaded her. "No. No," she finally said with a firm tone. "I used to be. That was a long time ago."

"Who are you trying to convince?"

"I—"

"Annie. You're still in love with Will. It isn't something you can pick or chose."

She blinked back unfamiliar emotions. "No. I can't be."

"Why not?"

"Because I've worked very hard not to be." An almost-hysterical laugh slipped out.

"Do you want to talk about it?"

"I couldn't. It seems a betrayal. Will is my best friend. We have no secrets." She stared down at the porch floor, her gaze taking in the scuffed toes of Ryan's boots as she spoke. "Suddenly I have a secret. There's something between us."

"Not so suddenly."

There was a long silence, before Annie could answer. "Maybe not." The words were a whisper.

"Will's a fool if he doesn't love you in return."

"Will doesn't have any interest in love or marriage."

"Ha. All men say that until they fall in love."

"It's different with Will." She struggled for words. "He has a, well, a painful history."

"Don't we all?"

Annie's gaze moved up to Ryan's handsome face, and she saw for a brief moment the sorrow and regret that touched his expression. He spoke from experience, she realized. "What are you going to do?" he asked quietly.

"There's nothing to do," Annie said.

"You could tell him."

"That would only make things uncomfortable and awkward. I don't want to ruin our friendship. It's too valuable."

"I disagree. Sometimes you have to take a chance. Win or lose, you can at least move on knowing you tried."

Annie inhaled. "It doesn't matter. I'm not going to be here all that much longer anyhow."

"You don't have to leave."

"I want a home of my own, and maybe if I keep moving I won't notice I can't have the one I really want."

"Don't be so sure. Someday you'll have that, and more."

"I wonder. It's not like I have a genetic predisposition toward home and hearth anyhow."

He scratched his head. "You know, I try to keep up on my medical reading, but I don't remember hearing about any test for that."

She tried to smile. "You know what I mean."

"You're selling yourself way short. Just remember that if you know in your soul that Will is the man you love, then you ought to know that God is who put that knowledge there."

Annie looked at Ryan, hope warming her from the inside out. *Could he be right?*

"But what about you?" The words slipped out before she could measure them.

"Me? Who's been talking about me?" Ryan asked, his tone light and jocular.

Annie wasn't fooled. "Rose mentioned your engagement," she said softly.

He was quiet for a moment, twirling his hat on his fingers. "Remember the talk the associate pastor gave at church tonight?" he asked.

She nodded. "Yes."

"Been thinking about it all evening myself."

"Me, too," she admitted. The thrust of the message had been that God wants His children to pursue His best for them and that included the context of a marriage partner. He discouraged his audience from rushing into marriage to end single life. God's best, whatever that path might be, was out there for each and every one of them, if they'd be patient.

"Annie, if the pastor is right, well, then all I can figure is that God's best must be there somewhere. I thought I'd found her once. I guess I was wrong, so I keep walking, one foot in front of the other. I keep focused on the fact that the last stop…"

He glanced down at her. "Well, that last stop is going to knock me off my feet, because that's what it's going to take at this point. I haven't given up hope. God's best. That's what I want."

Annie smiled, knowing Ryan was right. Knowing she'd already found her last stop.

Annie pushed open the screen door and poked her head inside. "Rose?"

"Marla just found out Lance cheated on her with her best friend. The wedding is off."

"She's too good for him."

"You got that straight. It's her own fault, too. You don't go looking for a stallion in a donkey corral."

Annie laughed. "Do you know where Will is?"

"He's helping Joanie and Chris exercise the horses."

"Do you think he'd mind if I took the Jeep down to the post office?"

"Take the truck," Rose said.

"Never touch a man's pickup."

"Don't be silly. Take the truck."

"No way. I'll be back in a bit."

"Marla threw the ring at Lance," Rose returned.

"Serves him right."

Annie tossed the keys in the air and slid into the Jeep. She slipped her stack of mail into the glove box and started the engine.

With a quick perusal left and right, she maneuvered out to the main road, then reached for the radio. The finicky dial was stripped and rewarded her with loud intermittent bursts of static. By the time she was a mile down the road she finally coaxed music out of the radio and began humming to the country tune.

Out of the corner of her eye she spotted a black-and-white skunk crossing the road. A quick jerk on the steering wheel averted a foul collision.

"We'll both be happier if I don't hit you, little guy." The Jeep veered off to the soft grassy shoulder, bumping over dead shrubbery before it stalled.

Annie watched the animal scurry into the trees as she shoved the clutch into Neutral. Turning the engine over again resulted in an unexpected grinding sound. The Jeep wasn't going to start. Had she flooded the engine? Too bad she knew even less about car mechanics than she did about skunks.

She leaned back against the worn seat cushion to wait it out. Her fingers slipped the visor down, and she curiously examined the yellowed scraps of papers tucked into the elastic band; a few receipts, a faded newspaper article covering the Tulsa State Fair. Rose's peach pie had won first place that year. Annie smiled. Between the pages of the newspaper clipping was a folded copy of her college graduation announcement. As she pulled it out a wrinkled business card tumbled to her lap.

"Neurologist?" *Who's seeing a neurologist?*

With a frown, she carefully replaced the business card and papers.

The next time she tried the engine it merely clicked repeatedly with her efforts, removing all doubt that she was going to have to walk back to the ranch. She glanced at the tree-lined road.

Obviously the skunk knew the shortcut. Cutting across the field would be a much shorter route than taking the road and the long driveway.

She pushed through the low-hanging branches and a dense tangle of bushes to a clearing. The Dearbornes had already erected a wood and double-line barbed-wire fence along the new property line.

Annie stared at the fence and sighed.

She tucked her left pant leg into her sock before pulling herself up onto the wooden post and lifting the injured leg over the barbed wire carefully. Just as she began to lift her right leg over the fence, the skunk reappeared.

A frantic scramble cleared her over the top of the wire; but when she tried to move forward, Annie realized she was still attached to the fence. Oh, she'd gotten over all right, but now she was standing on her tiptoes with her shirt caught on the sharp barbs.

Twisting her body, she glanced over her shoulder. The skunk's bright beady eyes mocked her.

"Shoo." She waved a hand.

Annie paused and tugged at her shirt. Oh, yes. She was pinned clear through to her undergarments. Facing off with a skunk and unable to escape.

"I said shoo. You little troublemaker."

Taking a deep breath, she fought to stay calm. "Skunks rarely attack. Skunks rarely attack." She repeated the mantra over and over.

"What are you doing?"

Will.

With the show over, the skunk trotted off into the trees.

"Your friend is leaving," Will observed.

"Darn."

"So how long have you been stuck to that fence?"

"Oh, not long." She gritted her teeth and tried again to yank herself free while maintaining a nonchalant appearance.

Will inched closer, bringing his face near as he assessed first her and then the barbed wire from his position on the other side. When his Stetson sailed past and landed on the grass on her side of the fence, Annie turned toward him and paused, mesmerized by the dark head close to her own. Her gaze moved to the shadowed stubble on his chin, and the firm lips. She shivered.

"Are you hurt?"

Oh, she was in pain all right. But she wasn't hurt.

"I'm just fine."

"Don't move or you'll put a hole in your shoulder blade." In one graceful movement he leaped over the wire.

"Put your arms around me."

Annie blinked. "I beg your pardon?"

"Now's not the time to be shy, Annie. Hold on to me and I'll get you free."

She put her arms around his neck, her fingers touching the soft curls at the base of his neck. Will smelled like a day's work—the musky scent of leather, hay and horses. For a brief moment she closed her eyes, imagining what it would be like to really be held in Will's arms.

With one hand he held her off the ground while his other hand freed the fabric. "Okay, got it."

She opened her eyes and found her mouth a mere breath from his.

"You okay?" His words were warm against her skin.

"I was." She sucked in a shaky breath and licked her lips.

He froze, his pupils dilated as he stared at her mouth. Finally he released her to slide down his chest and stand on the ground.

"Thank you," she muttered, staring at his boots while she straightened her dignity.

Will retrieved his hat and dusted it off against his

leg before setting it on the back of his head. "So, what were you doing out here?"

"Just hanging around."

The little laugh lines at the corner of his eyes appeared and Will began to chuckle. Doubled over, he apparently couldn't stop laughing.

"It's not that funny."

"Oh, yeah. It is." He straightened and fought for composure. "Annie, please don't ever leave."

For a moment her heart melted at the words she'd waited so long to hear. She released a small sigh of pleasure.

Then his lips twitched. "Life is so much more interesting with you around."

Annie narrowed her eyes and crossed her arms in front of her chest. "Glad I can amuse you."

Will cleared his throat. "Do you want to try that again?"

"I was on the way to the post office to mail my résumés."

"I like the sound of that. Jeep die on you?"

She nodded.

"Loose battery cables. I've got that on my list." He tossed her a set of keys. "Take the truck. I'll meet you back at the house. Oh, and I've got a jacket in there you can wear. Your shirt has a tear in it."

"I can't take your new truck."

"Annie, if I can't trust you with my truck, who can I trust?"

Chapter Thirteen

"Don't be silly," Rose said. "I want to go. I can sit long enough for a picnic. Just not on the ground." She examined the checkerboard situated in the middle of the kitchen table.

"What about fireworks?" Annie asked.

The older woman laughed. "Honey, I'll be asleep long before those fireworks start Sunday night."

"You can't go to bed early on the Fourth of July," Annie protested.

Rose returned a look that clearly stated "watch me" as she reached out to move her game piece.

Annie cleared her throat. "It's my turn."

"Well, then, quick talking and move."

It took all Annie's concentration to keep track of her own checker pieces and Rose's moves across the table. She jumped over a black and removed the piece from the board. "Okay, now it's your turn."

Rose stared at the board for several long minutes.

"You heard me say it's your turn, right?"

"You in a rush to lose?"

"But I'm winning," Annie said.

Rose slid her piece across the board. "Has Will got a group scheduled for the ranch that night?"

"No, I checked his schedule. Besides, he said he didn't want to deal with fireworks of any kind. Kids seem to pull them out of their pockets these days even though they're illegal."

After some thought Annie picked up another red piece. "King me."

Rose frowned.

"Maybe I'll give Ryan a call and see if he knows where we can see fireworks."

"No need to call Ryan. Will can tell you plenty of spots to view fireworks."

The phone rang, and Rose reached for the cordless handset that rested on the table between them. "Sullivan Ranch." When Rose arched her brows Annie guessed the caller to be Margaret. "Did you try his cell phone?" Her fingers tapped an impatient pattern on the table as she listened. "Hang on a minute. Let me ask his personal assistant."

"Is Will in the house?" Rose asked Annie with a grin.

"I think he's out with Okie."

"Could you fetch him?"

"Sure."

"Margaret, we'll have him call you right back," Rose said.

Annie stepped outside, and was immediately engulfed by the moist summer heat. She glanced around. The flowers were enjoying the humidity. The Boston ferns hanging on the porch were huge now, their lush, green fronds reaching out. They spanned at least three feet across. The deep ruby elephant's ears she'd planted along the front in the shade of the maple tree had grown as well, and also benefited from the moisture.

She stepped to the horse barn and pulled open the screen to the office. "Will?"

"Back here."

She found him in the tack room tidying up.

"Everything okay with your favorite mare?" she asked.

"Yeah, just getting the foaling kit together and giving Okie a rubdown. She's looking ready, isn't she?"

"Yes. I noticed that when I was helping Chris today." Annie wasn't any kind of horse expert, but she had learned the telltale signs of impending delivery from the vet tech.

"When Okie has her foal, that will be seven of your own and all the boarders. Aren't you excited?"

"Yeah. I am. A full house. Like the old days." He smiled, but a trace of melancholy laced his words.

"You're not selling the foal, then?"

"Don't know yet. Once upon a time that was the plan. Now I'm thinking otherwise."

"Wouldn't it be fun to have a foal around to raise and train? You'd enjoy that."

"You know me too well, Annie."

"What did the vet say today?"

"We're right on schedule."

"That's good news. Oh, I almost forgot why I came out here. Phone call. Margaret wants you to call her back right away. You forgot to take your cell off silent again."

He winced. "Think there's some kind of psychological thing going on there with me and cell phones?"

"Yes. Your subconscious wants the world to go away."

He sighed and moved out of the tack room to the office. "You're more right than you know." Turning out the light, he locked the door and followed her to the yard.

"Beautiful weather," he said.

"Hope it stays this way for the Fourth. I'm trying to convince Rose to go see the fireworks with me."

"Good luck. You should know better. This is the woman who is in bed by dusk on New Year's Eve. I can take you if you like."

"Really?" Excitement bubbled up inside of her. "What about Okie?"

"We'll set a monitor in here so Chris can listen to Okie from home."

Her eyes widened. *Will was really going to take a day off.*

"I'm thinking it might be fun to head out to an amusement park."

"Oooh, that's a great idea."

Will laughed. "You look like a five-year-old who was just offered cotton candy."

"I *feel* like a five-year-old."

"Good. 'Cause I like being the one putting those smiles on your face."

When his gaze met hers and she saw the earnestness in his eyes, her heart began to pound.

"There'll be a lot of walking."

She glanced down at her leg as they strode side by side toward the house. "I'm ready for it. It's not like we'll be in any rush."

"You're preaching to the choir. I'm always trying to keep up with you."

"I suppose I could slow down."

"Thanks."

"Wow, I haven't been to an amusement park in a long time. I want to ride Zingo." She hadn't been on the legendary wooden roller coaster in years.

"Sorry, Annie. Zingo is gone."

Annie inhaled sharply. "What?"

"Bells Amusement Park has closed."

"That's so sad. But you said amusement park."

"I thought we might take a ride to Oklahoma City and check out the new park there. Frontier City. They have a wooden roller coaster, too." He shrugged. "Still want to go?"

"Absolutely." She paused. "Just the two of us?"

"If that's all right with you."

"Yes. Of course," she said, suddenly shy. An unexpected pleasure filled her at the thought of an evening alone with Will. She might well enjoy her time here while she could.

"We'll take Rose home and head out right after the picnic."

Annie nodded as Will took the porch steps two at a time. "Coming?" he asked, holding the door.

"Go ahead. I'm going to water the pumpkins."

"Thanks for taking care of them," he said.

"You're going to have a pumpkin patch that will rival Linus's come September."

Will laughed as the screen door closed behind him.

Annie grabbed the sprinkler where it lay next to the coiled hose, wondering where she would be come September.

The notebook next to her bed listed the dates and locations for the viable mission teams for the next year. Mexico remained at the top of her list. She'd also received several job offers after her interviews. There were plenty of opportunities. The question was which one did the Lord want her to accept? She knew that if she chose the wrong path she'd be miserable, no matter how attractive the opportunity appeared.

Dragging the hose into the garden, she stooped down, positioning the head to reach the tender green vines that had taken over most of the garden. Then she backed out of the patch and turned on the faucet, standing to watch the whirring water pirouette and shoot into the night air.

Cast your cares on Him. Well, she had, and now she was simply waiting. And it wasn't easy. She'd come to see that perhaps she wasn't exactly restless like her mother, but she was impatient.

She removed her muddy sneakers before letting herself in the house, where she heard Will deep in conversation.

"Wish I could, Margaret, but I already have plans." Will tucked the portable between his ear and shoulder as he opened the refrigerator and perused the contents. Grinning, he pulled out a pie tin and set it on the counter. "Sure I understand. It sounds like a great party, and I appreciate you pulling strings to get me invited."

Rose rolled her eyes and shook her head, while Annie stared at the black and red game board.

"I'm trying to work with you, Margaret, but you have to give me some lead time for all these parties you have lined up. You know under any other circumstance I'd be happy to go to the country club with you and Ed for KidCare. But this is a holiday and I have plans."

"His nose is going to grow if he doesn't stop fibbing," Rose said.

"Will doesn't fib. What he means is that the circumstances under which he'd love to go to the country club would include impending natural disasters such as tornados or earthquakes. And he does have plans."

She smiled to herself. *Will had invited her out.*

Rose chuckled. "Know what his problem is?" she whispered. "Will is too nice for his own good. He's going to have to be up front with that woman eventually. She and Ed want him to be something he's not."

Annie gathered the checkers pieces and prepared for another round.

"That boy is going to end up miserable if he keeps trying to please everyone but himself."

"He's not a boy. He's a man, and we need to mind our own business."

Rose grumbled under her breath.

"Margaret, I've got to hang up now. I have an appointment to keep." He set down the phone and pulled out a plate from the cupboard. "An appointment with pie."

Will finished juggling the bills and closed his laptop. Why did he sense he was only a half trot ahead of disaster? So much depended on this summer. Time and again doubt snuck up, wooing him with words he didn't want to hear. Could he really save Sullivan Ranch, or was he only postponing the inevitable?

The photo of Annie on the corner of his desk caught his attention and he found himself smiling. Somehow thinking of Annie made even his anorexic bank statements seem less formidable. How could she always be so upbeat and positive? With a finger he swiped at a bit of dust on the glass frame.

His mind replayed that almost kiss in the pasture yesterday. He was only human and Annie was oh so tempting. But he refused to start something he couldn't finish, so he fought what he was feeling with everything in him.

The Huntington's set his boundaries long ago, but lately it was becoming more and more difficult to keep those fences in place. And the ache inside him was becoming a longing that he couldn't subdue with facts. Virtue was becoming its own punishment.

A groan escaped, and he pushed the thoughts aside and began to tidy up his desk. He glanced down at the list of suggestions for the ranch Annie had slipped on his desk yesterday.

It had been five weeks since he'd first offered up a prayer to make Annie stay. Had the Lord heard his prayers?

Will jumped at a thump in the darkness outside his office.

"Nuts."

"Annie?"

"Sorry. Didn't mean to disturb you." She peeked her head into the room and gave him a weak smile.

"What are you doing? It's after midnight."

"Well, I'm…um, I'm watching television. Are you aware they play reruns of Rose's soap opera late at night?" She stepped in the office, holding a butter knife, a jar of peanut butter, a soda and an apple in her hands.

"You're addicted to Rose's soap?"

"I wouldn't say that. But I have to find out what's going on with Lance and Marla."

Will barely suppressed a laugh. "I blame Rose for this. She's taking you to the dark side."

"Oh, come on. It's harmless."

"I'm not so sure."

"What are you doing?" She examined his desk. "Oh, my list. What do you think?" Her voice became hopeful.

"I haven't had a chance to really go over it yet."

Annie set her bounty on the desk and narrowed her eyes at him. "Look, Will, I know KidCare is putting a lot into marketing, but their focus is the events you sponsor with them. You need to get out there and market Sullivan Ranch. Your web page barely scratches the surface." She paced back and forth.

"Okay. Sure. We can work on that."

"Good, but what we really need to do is sit down and figure out what kind of packages the ranch can offer guests. I've been doing research, and you've got to round out your amenities. Maybe adding skeet shooting and horseback-riding trips with gourmet lunches on the side, and—"

"Annie, please don't leave." The words had burst from him before his brain could register what he'd done.

She stopped, closed her mouth and faced him, surprise leaving her momentarily speechless.

"I want you to work for me."

"But, but, I already work for the ranch."

"I meant with a paycheck. Part-time."

"You said you can't afford to hire anyone else."

"I can't afford not to hire you. You've been the difference between success and failure these past few weeks."

"You know that really isn't necessary. I love Sullivan Ranch. Besides, you and Rose have already given me so much."

"Still. I want to make it official."

When his gaze met hers, he saw her heart in her eyes and for a fleeting moment wondered if he was playing fair.

"Thanks, Will. That means a lot coming from you."

"It's nothing less than the truth. You have an amazing way to think outside of a situation and come up with a solution."

"Thank you," she said softly, glancing down at the floor.

"I hate to even ask. But maybe you could consider staying on for just a little while longer?" He took a deep breath. "Sullivan Ranch needs you."

Chapter Fourteen

"This way," Annie said, as they approached Wild-cat, the wooden roller coaster.

"I'm trying to keep up with you."

"Oh, I'm not going that fast."

"You're kidding, right?"

"Look. Isn't she beautiful?" Annie breathed, neck craned to take in the tracks and the white boards as she and Will stood next to the platform.

"Uh-huh. Those steel roller coasters are a dime a dozen. I love these old wooden coasters."

"This isn't Zingo, but it'll do."

Like most wooden roller coasters, Wildcat had limited seating. Unlike Zingo, which had one car, Wildcat had three cars holding up to eighteen passengers, two to a seat. Annie realized standing in line would be inevitable.

"You ready to ride?"

"Let's wait until the sun goes down," Annie said, excitement thrumming through her. "If we time things right, we'll be riding just when the fireworks begin."

Will smiled. "Okay, I'm willing. Though Lord knows I'm going to be exhausted tomorrow."

"That's not all you're going to be tomorrow. Look at your legs," Annie said. "You've already got a pink glow."

"I think today is the first time I've been in shorts all summer," Will commented. "Sunblock washed off when we were on the Renegade Rapids."

She dug in her tote bag and pulled out the sunscreen. "Here."

"Thanks."

White legs or not, Will looked wonderful, nothing like a formidable rancher with his casual attire of sneakers, khaki cargo shorts and dark blue T-shirt. The dark shirt showed off his muscled form, usually hidden by his ranch shirts. Hatless today, his dark hair was windblown, in disorder for a change. No, he wouldn't be mistaken for a rancher. He looked like every other hunky guy walking around the grounds. Except better. Much better.

Just remembering the feel of his dark curls beneath her fingers as he freed her from the barbed-wire fence left Annie shaky.

He grinned. "What are you thinking? Your eyes are sparking like there's trouble on your mind."

"Who? Me?" She laughed. "The church picnic was fun, wasn't it?"

"Sure was. I just want to know where Rose came up with those pies she brought."

"I'm not allowed to tell," Annie said. "That was awfully cool how Pastor Jameson took a turn at the dunking booth, don't you think?"

"Oh, yeah. I dunked him twice myself. All for charity, of course."

"Of course. Is that why you dunked Ryan?"

"A man's gotta do what a man's gotta do, Annie."

"So why didn't I see *you* up there?"

He scoffed.

"Look. Funnel cakes," Annie said, grabbing Will's arm and pulling him along toward a canopied trailer.

"You're going to have to pace yourself on this park food. I don't want you getting sick when we ride the roller coaster."

"I never get sick eating."

Will raised a brow.

"Wait a minute." She stopped right in the middle of the midway.

"Whoa." Will nearly ran into her backside, placing his hands on her waist to stop a collision. She tingled where he held her. "What now?"

"How did we miss the bumper cars?" she asked.

Will shoved his wallet back in his pocket. "I thought you wanted funnel cakes."

"That was before I saw the bumper cars. Come on, let's get in line." She frowned with impatience at a slow-moving young couple walking the midway in front of them who kept stopping to lip-lock.

"Good grief, that's ridiculous," she muttered under her breath, as the couple stopped yet again.

"You don't like PDA?"

"I prefer private displays of affection."

Will laughed. "Well, I learn something new about you every day."

Annie rolled her eyes and darted around them, her focus straight ahead.

"What's your rush?" Will asked from somewhere behind her.

Annie decreased her pace a fraction.

"Have you thought about getting funnel cakes and then getting in line?" he asked. "That line up there is long enough we'd have them done before we got to the front."

"That's an excellent idea."

"Hey, hey, just a second." He latched on to her hand as she spun around and pulled her close to his side. "You've got to quit taking off like that. I might lose you."

Annie smiled up at him. "Don't be silly. You aren't going to lose me."

Will watched Annie fight back sleep as she sat in the pickup, leaning against the huge stuffed penguin he had won at the arcade. On her lap was a plastic bag of partially eaten, neon-pink cotton candy. She blinked and crinkled up her face in a losing battle.

"That was so much fun." She yawned, and pushed her hair back over her shoulders.

It was, and he only wished he could have more days like today with Annie.

"You mean driving those bumper cars like a maniac?"

Will grinned as her embarrassed laughter filled the cab.

"Good thing I get to sleep in tomorrow," he commented.

She wiggled to sit up straight, and glanced at the clock on the dash. "I've got news for you. It *is* tomorrow."

"So it is."

"Besides, you never sleep in."

"I don't have to get up at five. That's sleeping in. I get to be lazy until seven. Chris is doing the morning rounds for me."

"I hope you won't regret taking off tonight."

"Never. Seeing the fireworks display while riding the roller coaster is a memory I'm not likely to forget."

The dark Oklahoma sky had provided a backdrop for nearly forty-five minutes of choreographed patriotic music and colorful explosions of color. Zipping high above the ground on the roller coaster, it seemed they could almost touch the stars overhead.

Nor would he forget Annie screaming with enthusiastic abandonment one moment, her hands lifted high in the air, and clutching his arm in fear the next, as the coaster suddenly dropped, taking their stomachs along with it.

It was just what the doctor ordered. Literally. He'd spent hours just having fun. Enjoying himself and his companion.

Will savored the memory of Annie's wicked expression as she knocked his bumper car, and her unpretentious delight at getting completely drenched as they rode the log flume. He'd forgotten the simple pleasure of the Ferris wheel as it took them to the very top of the world.

Will pulled the truck into the drive of Sullivan Ranch and turned off the engine, engaging the parking brake. He stretched his arms over his head. When his glance met Annie's in the darkened cab, he could have sworn she blushed.

"You've got powdered sugar on your face," he said.

"Do I?" With a nervous laugh she attempted to wipe it off, using her hand to rub her nose and cheeks.

"Completely missed." He chuckled. "Here let me." He leaned over to remove the white dust from her chin with the pad of his finger. As he connected with her skin he froze.

His eyes locked with hers.

Was that his Annie glancing at him so expectantly? Her lightly tanned face was framed by the curtain of her dark hair. The brown luminous eyes seemed even larger at this moment. Annie radiated light and beauty from the inside out. She was so lovely.

He hitched a breath looking down at her.

Slowly, his finger moved beneath her chin, nudging her face up.

She didn't resist.

Leaning forward, he paused, and time suspended for a moment, until Annie was the one to reach up to connect their lips. It seemed as natural as could be.

And then he was falling.

Falling into a kiss.

A butterfly kiss.

He might have imagined the whole thing except that her hand had crept up to gently caress his cheek, then his neck. No, he hadn't imagined that.

Will cleared his throat and gave his head a slight shake. "Annie," he breathed, unable to think rationally. Unable to put up defenses. In that moment it occurred to him that he had no defenses against this woman.

And he had no desire for defenses.

He longed to touch his lips to hers yet again, to see if he had imagined the intensity of one small kiss.

A tap on the window jarred him to reality. He and Annie both jumped.

"Will." Next to the driver's window stood Chris, looking harried. Will lowered the window.

"What's wrong, Chris?"

"I was just about to call you on your cell. It's Okie. Something's not right."

Will opened the truck door and hopped down. Annie did the same, withholding eye contact, not waiting for him to come around.

"You called the vet?"

"Couldn't reach him. But I'll keep trying. Called Ryan, he's on his way."

Together the three of them strode to the barn.

"I think we have a breech on our hands," Chris said, hands tucked in his pockets "She's been agitated the past hour, pacing around. I've stayed back watching. Then about fifteen minutes ago she started rolling around."

"Trying to reposition herself," Will stated.

"Yeah, that's what I thought."

Will shook his head. "Doesn't it just figure? Poor Okie." He went to the mare's stall and stood outside. Okie whinnied and paced, almost frenzied. He knew she was not herself right now and decided to maintain a distance and save agitating her further until Ryan arrived. "I better go change clothes. I'll be right back."

Annie followed him out of the barn, still carrying the stuffed penguin. "Would I be in the way if I changed my clothes and came to help?" she asked, eyes wide.

"You'd never be in the way, Annie," he said, trying to gauge her emotions. What a fix this was. There was no time to think. No time to talk. Okie needed them.

Lights of a pickup truck moved over them as they stood in the yard.

"Ryan," Annie said.

"The cavalry has arrived," Ryan called out, slamming the door of his beat-up pickup behind him. He'd obviously been asleep; his clothes were disheveled and his baseball cap was askew. From his right hand dangled a black leather satchel. "Ah, it's good to be needed."

"About time you got here, Jones," Will muttered.

"Hey, buddy, after we have our foal, we've got some unfinished business," Ryan said, striding up the drive.

"What are you jabbering about, Doc?" Will asked.

"Short memory, huh, Sullivan? That was me you dunked twice before you disappeared from the picnic. I call that foul play."

"So why are you complaining? First good bath you've had in a month."

Beside him, Annie choked on a laugh.

"Just wait. The time of reckoning is coming," Ryan said, as he headed into the barn. "I only hope I'm around when it happens."

Will grinned as he mounted the porch steps and unlocked the door. "We'll be right back," he called, as he held the screen door open for Annie.

"Better hurry. If she delivers before you get here, I get first dibs on naming the foal." He laughed. "I like the name Jonesy."

"That'll be the day," Will retorted.

When they entered the house, Annie dashed down the hallway ahead of him.

"Annie," he said, his voice low to avoid waking Rose, "we've got to talk."

She turned back, hugging the black-and-white toy to herself defensively, her gaze still avoiding his.

"Do I need to apologize for kissing you?"

Slowly and warily, her glance moved from the rag rug she'd been examining to his boots and, finally, she met his eyes. "I don't know. Do you?"

"I don't want to. I'd do it again in a heartbeat."

Okie's pained whinny filled the air.

"Will, everything all right?" Rose called from upstairs.

"It's Okie, Rose. Start praying." He glanced toward the barn then back to Annie. "We've got to get moving. But you need to know this isn't finished, Annie," he said. "Not by a long shot." He raced up the stairs to throw on his jeans, knowing his words sounded as frustrated as he felt.

Chapter Fifteen

The moment the silver-gray Mercedes sports coupe pulled up the long drive, Will started praying.

Not today.

He checked his watch, hardly believing it could be 9:00 a.m. already. After hard work and prayer, the drama of last night had ended on a positive note. Okie and her foal were resting. Only moments before, Ryan Jones's pickup had departed the spot the Benz now occupied.

He wasn't expecting Margaret, which could only mean trouble.

Will glanced down at his clothes. He was a fine mess. Between hay, horses, grease and sweat, he probably stank worse than the muck heap. Since he hadn't known she was coming, he figured she would have to take him as is. Period.

By the time Margaret got out of the car, sunglasses in place, back straight with purpose, Will realized with certainty the Lord wanted him to deal with the problem of Margaret Reilly right now.

Apparently so did she.

She fairly marched up the drive in her slim white suit and heels, a briefcase in one hand, a purse in the other. Her hair had been pulled into a no-nonsense Margaret-do, at the back of her head.

It might only be 9:00 a.m., but already the day threatened to be a scorcher. Will had to give her credit. The woman looked cool and fresh.

At the sight of him, she stopped. "What on earth happened to you?" Pulling her large tortoise-shell shades down a notch, she gave him a second assessment, wrinkling her nose before sliding the sunglasses back in place.

"Just another day on the ranch," Will answered drily. Removing his faded, old straw Stetson, he ran the sleeve of his shirt over his perspiration-streaked forehead before shoving the hat back on his head. He narrowed his eyes. "Was I expecting you?"

Her perfectly arched brows lifted in surprise behind the sunglasses. "Excuse me?" she said.

He hadn't meant to be rude, so he corrected himself. "What I meant was did we have an appointment that I forgot about?"

"I called the house several times yesterday afternoon and I left messages on your cell phone."

"It was a holiday, Margaret. I already explained to you that I had plans."

"KidCare needs to be able to reach you at all times."

Will patted himself down, but there wasn't a phone

on him. "Must have left it in the truck. And I did return your calls. I got your machine."

"You didn't leave a message."

He shrugged. No use explaining that besides being a little busy since she'd last seen him, he just refused to play phone tag.

He wasn't going to give Margaret his itinerary for every single hour of every single day, as she preferred. She ought to know that KidCare had booked him heavily for the summer, and if his weekends were free it was because his weekdays were accounted for with programs. Grateful for the business didn't come close to describing his appreciation. He had a job to do, and dealing with Margaret's machinations wasn't something that figured into his plans.

"Will, I'm here because I really think we need to talk."

"I'm filthy. I can't sit in the house until I shower."

"The porch is fine."

He eyed her. "Right now?"

"Do you have other plans?"

Oh, yeah, he could think of a dozen things that needed to be done, not to mention grabbing a few hours' sleep and taking a shower.

As he began to answer, Annie limped from around the corner and started up the steps. Exhaustion radiated from every inch of her bedraggled appearance, but she was still smiling, high from the birthing experience. Noting Margaret standing on the porch, she stood straighter, shoving her braid over her shoulder.

"Goodness, you're a mess," Margaret said.

Will shook his head. Leave it to Margaret to state the obvious.

"Think so?" Annie said, assessing Margaret's appearance as she clearly bit back annoyance. "I'm going to have to demand a raise. This personal assistant stuff is a lot more work than I thought I was signing up for."

He held back a smile.

Margaret sniffed the air and stepped back, fanning herself with a manicured hand. "What is that horrendous odor?"

Annie glanced down at herself, lifting one foot, and then the other. "Oops. Looks like I stepped in something mucking out the stalls." She shrugged and slipped off her sneakers, tossing them over the rail, next to the hose. "Pardon me," she said, pulling open the front door.

Will chewed his lip trying not to laugh.

"What is going on around here?" Margaret asked Will as the screen door slammed.

"Okie delivered last night," Will stated.

"I see," Margaret said. "Everything went as expected?"

"Not exactly, but we've got it under control now."

Will motioned to the wicker chairs in the far corner of the wraparound porch. Annie had recently helped Rose order the pair from the Sears catalog. He had to admit they looked inviting on the porch.

"Sometimes you can catch a breeze over there,"

he said, attempting to keep the resigned edge out of his voice. "And for your sake, I sure hope I'm downwind."

Margaret sat, removed her sunglasses and placed her briefcase on the gray-painted floorboards of the porch. "Rose has done a lovely job on the flowers and plants," she said, her gaze taking in the huge Boston ferns overhead and the basket of bright purple petunias on the railing.

"Annie did that. She has Rose's green thumb."

Margaret bristled. "Ah, yes, Annie."

The silence stretched until Will couldn't take any more.

"Let me wash my hands and get us some ice water." He stood without waiting for an answer.

Thankfully, Rose was already gone to an outing with Ellen and their bridge group. She'd almost stayed behind, until Annie had convinced her Ryan had everything under control with the horses and she should go as planned.

He heard the shower upstairs, indicating Annie wasn't within earshot. Sudsing his hands and rinsing, Will sluiced water over his face and neck, drying off with a wad of paper towels. He downed a quick cup of black coffee before preparing two glasses of ice water and heading outside.

"Thank you," Margaret murmured at his offered glass.

She reached down and opened the leather briefcase at her feet. "I have those advertising contracts for you to sign. I need them as soon as possible so we can get the print ads going and the radio spots."

"Okay." Will said the words slowly. He'd already told Ed that he'd stop by the KidCare offices Tuesday to sign them.

"I'm also working on a guest appearance for you on one of the Christian talk radio shows."

Will winced. He'd have to speak to Ed about that particular idea. He'd agreed to be less resistant to Margaret's ideas, but thought of a talk show was enough to make him queasy all over.

Still standing, he wiped his right hand on the back of his Wranglers before taking the pen Margaret offered with the paperwork. That done, he handed everything back. "That all?"

"Could you sit down, please?"

"Sure," he agreed as he fingered the condensation on his glass.

"When will Annie be leaving?"

"Never, I hope. This is Annie's home."

"No." She said the word carefully. "It is not. It's your home. You're very generous to keep Rose here, and to allow Annie to stay, but it is, after all, Sullivan Ranch."

Will cleared his throat. "What's your point, Margaret?" he asked, irritation beginning to steal the upper hand.

"That is my point, Will. Sullivan Ranch is no longer a mom-and-pop operation. You've moved past that."

"Okay. Great."

"What will happen when you get married?"

"Pardon me, but is that any of your business?"

"For the sake of this discussion, could you simply answer the question?"

"I'm not getting married. Period."

"You say that with such finality, but things do change. No wife will be eager to share her home with two other women."

"That's moot, since I told you I am not getting married."

Margaret stared at him, as though regrouping.

He took a deep breath and tried to be gentle. "The fact is, Margaret, I don't understand. What are we talking about here? Our business agreement doesn't give you a free hand in my personal life."

Margaret stood and began to pace the porch. She stopped and frowned, her attention wholly on Will.

Will met her gaze straight on.

"Will, you agreed to work with me on the marketing plans for this joint venture. As Ed reminded you, that means expanding your networking."

"Okay."

"You bowed out of last night's event."

He knew this was the real issue on Margaret's mind. Knew it as surely as he knew every inch of Sullivan Ranch.

Will sucked in his breath and prepared himself.

"You weren't listening. I said I had plans last night."

"Plans with Annie."

"You best cut to the chase, Margaret."

She turned and faced him. "Will, it's been six weeks since Annie arrived, and this situation has gotten out of hand. Things have gone from a nagging suspicion to the obvious."

"Obvious what?" And if what she was talking about was so obvious, why didn't he have a clue what she was getting at?

Ignoring him, she continued her monologue, raising a hand to her cheek in a dramatic gesture. "I didn't want to believe it, but one of my friends called me last night. She saw you in OK City with Annie. You were holding her hand."

This time it was Will who jumped to his feet. He shook his head, thinking he couldn't have possibly heard her correctly. "You have friends monitoring me or something?"

"There are serious repercussions if you don't think this situation through. I am not claiming any impropriety on your part, Will. You are an honorable man. But if I have had these concerns then others will, too."

"Are you saying you think…" He narrowed his eyes and stared at Margaret as though he'd never seen her before. For a moment he wished he hadn't.

"We have to be held to a standard, or both Kid-Care and Sullivan Ranch may suffer."

His stomach turned, and he couldn't speak. For the first time in years anger had a hold of him, and the emotion was so powerful, he was unable to utter a word.

Lord. Help me not to react.

Forcing calmness, he reached for his glass and downed the water. With great care, he set the glass on the floor fearing he might break the vessel with his bare hands.

Control. He must get himself under control—for Annie's sake, for his sake and for the future of Sullivan Ranch.

Clenching and unclenching his hands, he breathed slowly, eyes focused on the white clapboard of the porch shutters. He'd learned relaxed breathing years ago after researching Huntington's.

Emotional instability was not uncommon with progression of the disease. So he'd trained himself to stay in control. The lessons would serve him now.

Turning, he faced Margaret. He heard his voice, sounding as cold as the ice that had chinked in his water glass a moment before. "I think you'd better leave now. I have chores to finish before tonight's youth program."

Annie staggered back from the door. Legs weak, she leaned against the wall, her heart performing wild palpitations.

What had she just heard? Margaret's accusations left her emotions tearing back and forth between shock and grief. Dumbfounded by the woman's words, Annie remained frozen in the hallway.

The ranch meant everything to Will. The possibility that she herself could hurt the reputation of

Sullivan Ranch and cause Will to lose his dreams nauseated her.

She closed her eyes for a moment as Will's follow-up words rang in her head. *He would never marry.* The pain inflicted by his words was no less stunning now than the first time she'd heard the same words years ago, only affirming how foolish she was.

There was no way she could face Will without him guessing that she had overheard the entire conversation.

It had been innocent enough. She'd come down-stairs after her shower and heard Margaret's voice as she walked past the open door. She'd moved forward to close the oak door and keep the cool air-conditioning from escaping through the screen. But, it was the sound of her own name being bandied about in angry tones that had frozen Annie to the spot.

She almost wished she'd taken longer upstairs.

Almost.

Gathering every bit of reserve strength and bitter resolve, she lifted first one leg and then the other, and walked the long path, down the hall to her room at the other end of the house. Closing the door, she turned the lock.

The midmorning sun streamed in through the window as though nothing was amiss with the day. As though her entire world had not been turned upside down.

Annie glanced around the comforting surround-ings as if for the last time. She ran a loving hand over the quilt, then walked to the window and closed the blinds against the sunshine, cloaking the room in darkness.

Margaret had one thing right. This wasn't her home. She wasn't a child anymore. It was more than time to stop pretending.

Stripping off her clothes, she slipped on her pajamas. The sheets were cool and welcoming as she slid beneath the quilt, plumping the pillow under her face. Hot tears slid silently from her eyes, to be caught by linens.

She was lying to herself and she couldn't do it any longer.

Yes, she loved Will.

She always had and always would.

The truth was Will did not return her love. She touched her lips with her fingers. Could it be more plain and simple? She was good enough to kiss but not good enough to marry. No matter how many times she tried to see it from another angle, those were the facts.

It was time to get on with her life. Find a life was more like it.

Since she'd been back at the ranch many of the issues in her spirit had been settled. She wasn't her mother. She'd proved that in Kenya. Proved that in the nursery on Sundays and proved it here on the ranch.

No, she did not have a restless heart. And someday the Lord would provide her with a partner who was her own God's best.

For a moment her thoughts turned to Ryan Jones,

and she understood the words he'd shared. "Keep walking," he'd said. "One foot in front of the other. Keep focused on the last stop."

Until then, she needed to concentrate on the doors that had opened for her. She had choices. She wouldn't run through them, as Will accused. No, she would pray and find God's direction for her life.

Yes, it seemed everything was falling into place. She could see clearly now. Wiping her eyes, she reached for a tissue from the bedside table.

Inching over to the edge of the mattress, she stretched her hand past the eyelet skirt and under the bed, rummaging for the packet she'd stuffed beneath weeks ago.

She pulled the envelope out and shoved it under her pillow. "Lord, direct me," she prayed.

The banging on her door had Annie out of the bed and sitting on the floor in a tangle of covers before she could figure out what had happened. Disoriented, she glanced around. The room was bathed in darkness.

"Hey, Annie, I need your help. Got a sick kid outside," Will yelled through the heavy oak door.

"What time is it?" she called.

"Eight-thirty."

"In the morning?"

"No, at night. Could you hurry up?"

"Okay, okay. Give me two minutes."

She threw on the clothes she'd tossed on the

floor hours earlier and pulled her hair back into a haphazard ponytail.

Jerking open the door, she faced Will, blinking at the bright light of the hallway. "What's the emergency?" she growled, as she tucked her shirt into her jeans.

"Morning, Annie Sunshine," he said. Will leaned against the wall, a black Stetson on his head. He wore new jeans and a black polo shirt with the Kid-Care emblem on the pocket. "You look like you were run over by a tractor."

He might sound cheery, but his bloodshot eyes gave him away. It had been a rough twenty-four hours for both of them.

"Thank you," she said through gritted teeth. "Where'd you get the spiffy duds?"

Will glanced down at himself and turned red. "Margaret's idea. I look like a mail-order cowboy, don't I?"

"I'm sure it grows on you."

"Great." He pushed the hat back an inch. "You were tired, huh?"

"Exhausted. Now where's your problem child?"

"On the front porch. I was afraid to let him in the house, he's already thrown up all over the campsite. This is actually a doubleheader."

"Can you bring me the first-aid kit?" Annie asked, as she moved past Will to the front hall and out the screen door.

A thin boy of about twelve sat on the wicker settee, resting his head against the house. It was nearly dusk, and the porch light served to emphasize his pallor.

Across from him on the porch steps sat a pudgy kid of about the same age, who scratched at his legs continually to the point of drawing blood.

"Hi, I'm Annie. I'm a nurse."

The thin child nodded. The other grimaced and kept itching.

Annie sat down on the settee. "You are…?"

"Henry."

"Mind if I do a quick check and ask you a few questions?"

He raised his head and nodded.

"Henry, did you feel okay before you came to the retreat?"

He nodded affirmative again.

"Do you have any allergies?"

"No."

The screen door opened and Will handed her the kit along with two pieces of paper. "Medical releases and information."

Glancing at the information on the paper, Annie removed the oral thermometer from its container, shook it down and sheathed it in a plastic cover.

"Under your tongue. No talking until it beeps," she instructed Henry as she perused his information sheet, finding nothing out of the ordinary.

She donned a pair of latex gloves she sat down next to the other boy. "You are?"

"Chad."

"Got into a little poison ivy, Chad?"

"I guess."

"How did it happen?"

Chad shrugged. "I was hiding in the bushes. Minding my own beeswax."

"I don't think Chad is telling you the entire story," Will interrupted. "The bushes he is talking about are on the other side of the orchard. Way out of bounds."

Chad studiously examined the soiled laces on his sneakers. "I was just minding my own beeswax, I tell you."

The thermometer beeped.

"Would you get that, Will?"

"Normal."

"Thanks. And could you grab a couple of old washcloths and put some warm water and soap on them? Chad here needs to wash that oil from the poison ivy off his legs."

"Is that gonna make the itch stop?" Chad asked.

"Probably not. You're not contagious, but you're going to have a lousy week until the itching subsides. I think you'll be more comfortable at home." She glanced up at Will. "Did you call his parents?"

"They're on the way. They were relieved we have a nurse on duty."

She took the washcloths from Will and handed them to Chad. "Gently," she said. "It won't do any good to remove the skin."

Annie stood. "Let me wash my hands before I check out Henry."

Will followed her into the kitchen. "Thanks, Annie. I don't know what I would have done without you here."

"Chad's parents are right. You do need a full-time nurse out here," she said, as she scrubbed her hands and arms.

"I've got you."

She snorted and moved deftly past him, back outside. "You think you've got me," she mumbled. "We're going to have to negotiate my contract very soon."

Will groaned. "Why is it I don't like the sound of that?"

She moved past Will outside. "What did you eat tonight?" she addressed Henry.

"Six hot dogs, four bags of chips and a bunch of marshmallows."

Annie looked him up and down wondering where he hid it all. "Anything else?"

He shook his head.

"You forgot to mention the earthworm," Will added.

"Earthworm?" Annie nearly gagged, as did Henry.

"The men were trying to gross out the women. Looks like it might have backfired," Will said.

"Are you still nauseated?" Annie asked. "Because I know I am just thinking about it."

"Not much. Lots better since I threw up."

"Well, I think you're going to live. The worm is probably a goner, though. We'll need to call your parents and update them. Do you want to stay the rest of the night?"

"I have to, or the guys will think I'm a..." His voice trailed off.

"Sure, I know," Annie said, commiserating. "No more food tonight. I'll send you back with some ginger ale. You sip on that. Okay?"

"Henry, come with me," Will said, nodding toward the house. "We'll call your folks, make sure they're okay with you staying."

Annie followed them, pulling two cans of ginger ale out of the refrigerator and handing them to the boy. "Sip. Do not gulp. Got it?"

Henry nodded.

"And no more you-know-what," she added.

"Thanks, Annie," Will said, handing Henry the phone after talking to his parents.

"Earthworm?" she repeated with a shudder.

"Yeah. New one on me, too."

Will paced back and forth as a strained silence developed in the kitchen while they waited for Henry to finish his call. Annie bit her lip, irritation consuming her. They'd never had this sort of tension between them before, and she absolutely hated it.

"Um, Rose got back okay?" she asked, hoping to bring things back to a normal balance.

"Yeah," he answered, still not giving her eye contact. "We figured you were sleeping. She did her therapy and went to bed about a half hour ago."

"You get any sleep?" Annie couldn't help but ask.

"Took a nap. I'm okay."

"How's Okie and the foal?"

"Doing fine. The vet can't be here until the morning, so Ryan came back and did a check on them. He asked about you."

"Ryan?"

"Yeah. Told him you were sleeping."

Annie nodded, looking everywhere except at Will's eyes. He took off his cap, slapped it back on and glanced over at Henry. She watched Will watch Henry.

The moment Henry hung up the phone, Will and the boys climbed into the Jeep. "Going to take Henry back to camp and get Chad's sleeping bag and stuff. I'll be right back," he said.

Annie said nothing. She fully intended to grab something to eat and hide in her room.

Chapter Sixteen

Now would be the obvious time to tell them. Annie passed the tossed salad to Rose and the rolls to Will.

"Rose, this meal is delicious. You outdid yourself," Annie said. It never hurt to grease the pan before you got started. Rose herself taught her that. "Were the greens from your garden?"

"They were. Tomatoes and onions, too. I wouldn't have had a garden at all this year if you hadn't stepped in and taken care of things, Annie. Don't think I don't appreciate your help."

She smiled back, still waiting for the right opening.

"Does my heart good to see how your appetite has improved since you got home. You've put back on a couple pounds, haven't you?"

"Five, and that's plenty."

"Well, you look good." She glanced over to Will. "Doesn't Annie look good, Will?"

"Hmm?" Will said. He glanced back and forth at

the two women. "Yeah, everything is looking good. The chicken-fried steak is delicious. Any more of these rolls?"

"On the stove," Rose said. When Will got up, she shook her head and leaned close to Annie. "Don't mind him. He's been chomping at the bit all week. Cranky and irritable. Distracted, too. Can't figure out what's going on, but I imagine eventually he'll tell us."

Annie doubted he'd confide in her. In fact, in the past week they hadn't even been in the same room together except once or twice, for brief moments.

Yes, she had been avoiding Will.

Or maybe it was the other way around. Was he avoiding her?

Certainly she didn't have the experience to know how a woman acted after a life-altering kiss by the man she was in love with. Was nonchalance the appropriate response? Annie sighed.

Either way, she ached for him. He'd endured a staggering week at the ranch, every moment filled with a new problem. First one of the tractors broke down out in the north forty and had to be towed to town, then a double booking—Margaret's error— had to be sorted out.

So if Will seemed a bit preoccupied this week, she understood.

Annie wasn't sleeping well herself. She lay awake at night worried about Margaret's threats and the future of the ranch. Will was on precarious ground his first season, and Annie refused to be the straw that would make Will's dream come tumbling down.

"Did you see that announcement in the paper?" Rose asked.

"What announcement?" Annie asked.

"Lulu Parson's wedding. She and Howard Reynolds are getting married at the end of the month."

"That was quick," Will said, cutting the last of his meat.

"At her age I don't suppose she has any time to waste," Rose said.

"I think it's sweet. I hope we're invited to the wedding," Annie said.

"Me, too, so long as we don't do yoga at the reception." Rose laughed.

"Speaking of the end of the month," Annie said, her voice squeaky and off-key. She picked up her tea and took a long swallow, then cleared her throat.

Rose raised her brows.

Will finished chewing and swallowed, eyes on Annie. "Why am I pretty sure you're fixing to spoil my appetite?"

Ignoring him, she continued. "I've made a few decisions and I want to share them with you all."

Annie took a deep breath, praying for strength. "I've decided to accept the short-term medical mission position outside of Mexico City."

Will dropped his fork. "You agreed to stay and help with the ranch less than a week ago." He pinned her with his gaze, and the pretty speech she'd planned left her.

"I'm sorry, Will, but I think it's for the best. And it's two weeks away."

"Best for who?" he stated, his intense gaze never leaving her.

If only she could read what was going on in his head, but his expression remained hooded.

"I decided this was too good an opportunity to pass up. And it's just a short trip."

"Define 'short trip,'" he said.

"A one-year commitment with the option to stay longer," Annie said slowly.

"There's a flaw in your math. Two weeks is a short trip. Not a year," he said.

A knock at the front screen door interrupted them. "Anybody home?"

Annie jumped up, grateful for Ryan's appearance. "Come on in. We're in here."

Ryan Jones stuck his head out from around the corner and shot Will an evil grin.

"And what are you doing here? Every time I look up I see your ugly mug."

"Watch it, Sullivan. I'm giving serious thought to raising my rates. You haven't gotten my consultation bill on Okie's delivery yet. I ought to double it since I've had to put up with your rotten attitude all week." Ryan removed his hat. "And since you asked so nicely, Annie invited me for pie."

Will glared as Ryan smiled at Annie.

"Glad you could stop by, Ryan," Rose said, sounding for once glad to see the vet. She pulled out the chair between her and Will and set another plate on the table. "Don't listen to Will. He's got a burr in his Wranglers tonight. Some folks don't appreciate what's in front of them as much as others."

"Isn't that the truth, Ms. O'Shea?" Ryan responded, sitting down.

"What are you talking about?" Will asked, glancing at Rose and Ryan, confusion on his face.

"Did you want peach or blackberry? Take your pick," Rose said.

"Could I have both?" Ryan asked. "No way to choose between two such delicious offerings." He winked at Annie, who held back a laugh.

"Oh, what a load of cow pies," Will said, shaking his head.

"A smart man," Rose said. "He knows how to keep the peace."

"If he's so smart, how come he isn't telling Annie not to go off to Mexico?"

"You decided on Mexico?" Ryan leaned his chair back and looked to Annie.

Annie nodded as she placed clean glasses and a jug of milk on the table. Their eyes connected and Ryan gave her a sad smile of understanding.

"You have to do what your heart tells you. I understand that," Ryan said.

Will headed for the barn, feeling tied up in knots and not understanding why. Everything seemed to be coming at him at once, and he flat out did not have the time or the energy needed to sort it all out.

In one short week his orderly life had spiraled out of control and he felt powerless. First Margaret. Now Annie.

He blamed himself for what happened with Margaret. He should have set Ed and Margaret straight long ago. Rose was right. They had stepped over the line, and somehow gotten the idea they were running his life and Sullivan Ranch.

Things had been so crazy there hadn't been a minute to sort out the other night with Annie.

What got into him that night? For the first time in a very long time, he was just a normal guy out with a girl. Not a man with Huntington's hanging over him. And like an ordinary guy, he gave in to what his heart told him.

What had his heart said that night?

It didn't matter. He would not allow himself to even explore his feelings for Annie. To go there would be disaster.

Annie above all others deserved better. She deserved a whole man and a home with children.

Not a fifty-fifty man.

The more he thought, the more confused he became. Right or not, Margaret's words had hit home.

His world had changed in the six short weeks since Annie returned. He wasn't worried about the ranch, but he wouldn't do anything to slander Annie's reputation.

'Course now Annie had taken everything out of his hands by deciding to leave. He couldn't help but wonder at the timing. Had she made a prayerful decision, or was she running on impulse again? Had Margaret spoken to Annie, too?

"What's the story, Sullivan?"

Ryan stood next to him at Okie's stall, arms folded over the gate. Will hadn't even heard him come into the barn.

"Don't mess with me, Doc."

"You need some messing with." As he spoke Okie came over, recognizing the vet. Ryan pulled a small apple from his pocket and held it in his extended palm for the mare.

Apparently his horse had traded allegiance, too.

"Relax," Ryan said. "Ms. O'Shea sent me out here. Figured you need a little *mano-y-mano*."

"Rose said that?"

"Yep."

Will burst out laughing, the tension eased by Ryan's words. "You have no idea what it's like living in a hormone-dominated house."

"Yeah, you're breaking my heart. The only thing fighting for domination at my house are a Siamese and a German shepherd."

"Don't I hear your mother calling you?"

Ryan chuckled. "You decide if you're keeping the filly?"

Will's gaze took in the small, chocolate-brown horse with the spindle legs standing next to her mother. Her sleek coat was the exact same color as Annie's hair. The big, dark eyes the same color as Annie's eyes. "She stays."

"Annie-O, huh?"

Will nodded.

"So tell me again, why it is you're giving Annie a hard time?"

"Not that it's any of your business, but I'm giving her a hard time because she belongs here. Plain and simple. Sullivan Ranch is her home."

"That's not how she sees the situation. She'd like a home of her own."

Ryan turned and stood with his back against the gate to look Will up and down, apparently not particularly liking what he saw.

"What the hay are you talking about?" Will asked. "I just said this is her home."

"That's not how she sees it."

A good day was when everything went just the way he planned. A bad day was when things were out of his control. Yesterday had been one lousy day.

Will shook his head as he moved down the stairs with heavy steps and headed to the kitchen. A small lamp was on in the living room, bathing the room in an amber glow. He glanced at the clock on the mantel. Only 3:00 a.m., and here he was awake again. You'd think he'd have been exhausted after all the riding he did yesterday afternoon.

After Annie's announcement he couldn't face going back to the house, and he had taken one of the horses out and rode until they both were tired. By then it was nearly nightfall.

Confusion had left little room for anything such as sleep last night.

The kitchen light was on, and he was surprised to see Rose at the table, her Bible and a cup of tea in front of her. She wore her robe and fuzzy slippers.

"Morning, Will. Couldn't sleep either?"

"No, a lot on my mind."

"I imagine."

"Where's your walker?" he asked, dodging her last words.

"I've been set free by the therapist," she said.

"Good for you. I'm proud of how hard you've worked these weeks, Rose."

"Couldn't have done it without Annie. Her being here when I fell made all the difference."

"Yeah, you're right."

"Timing is everything, Will. Remember that."

Will stared at her, his head cocked. Where did that come from? And why did it seem like everyone was talking in double entendres these days?

He was having a hard time keeping up. For now he chose to stay in the dark. So again he evaded her words, instead taking a peach from the bowl on the table. He rubbed his thumb over the soft, ripe fruit and bit in. The sweet flavor burst in his mouth.

"Having a good yield this year," he commented, reaching for a napkin. "If I bring a few more bushels up from the orchard, will you have time to work on them?"

"Ellen is coming by to help me this weekend.

Between us, and with Annie's help, we'll get them canned and frozen. Thinking about jam, too."

"Love your jam."

"Thank you. Maybe you could run a few bushels by the parsonage?"

"I'll do that," he said.

"You're a good boy, Will," Rose said.

"Ma'am?"

"I said you're a good boy. Always have been. Pig-headed, and stubborn like your daddy. But a good heart."

"Uh, thank you." Rose was acting a little strange this morning. He gave her the benefit of the doubt, knowing sometimes she got sentimental for no reason. "Mind if I fix a bowl of cereal? I don't want to disturb you," he asked.

"Oh, you aren't disturbing me. In fact, I imagine you and I are way overdue for a little chat. Seems like a good time, since we're both awake."

"Rose, can I be honest here?"

She nodded.

"I've had more 'little chats' this week than I think I have had in my entire life. They're wearing on me. One more thing turns me upside down and I don't know what I'm going to do."

Rose smiled serenely. "That so? Then I guess you better make a pot of coffee, too. And make it real strong, son."

Chapter Seventeen

Will took a shower while the coffee perked, hoping it might prepare him for his chat with Rose. One way or another, for the past ten years he'd known that eventually this day would come.

He sat down across from her, hands warming on the mug of fresh coffee, leaning forward to inhale the bracing aroma.

Rose wasted no time. "You have to tell her."

While her words brooked no argument, he disagreed, knowing exactly who she referred to.

"With all due respect, Rose, I can't do that." He shook his head. Sure it was pride, but he simply could not handle the thought of Annie pitying him. Or worse, what if she decided to stay at the ranch because of the Huntington's? Deep inside he died a little at that thought.

"I've never pushed you. I've let you handle this your own way, in your own time. All I've done is pray. Pray the good Lord would give you wisdom.

I think ten years is plenty long to wait on the Lord, don't you?"

"Ma'am?" Will didn't have much to say to that.

Rose continued, obviously not needing an answer. "There are a few things you need to know before you completely shut the door." She removed her glasses and wiped a trace of moisture from her eyes.

"Rose," Will said softly. He could not stand for her to be upset.

She closed her eyes for a moment. "Listen. Hear me through."

He nodded, sighing.

"Your father's life was a prison of his own making, Will. He refused to allow anyone to know about the Huntington's. Time and again he refused the very medication which could have at least helped him. He refused to let anyone in, not even you and I. At the end his life was shortened, not expanded, by his stubborn pride.

"Don't get me wrong. I understand Huntington's as well as you do. I researched it plenty during those years. There was no test for Huntington's while your father was alive, but that's no excuse. I know the final result would have been the same. But things could have been much different day to day, if he would have just bent a little."

She took a steadying breath. "Pride is a dangerous thing, Will. Because he barely allowed treatment for any of his symptoms, Bill gave in to the disease. He lost hope right from the start."

There was nothing Will could say to Rose. She was absolutely right.

"You were six when he hired me. At that time the tremors and the memory problems had already begun. Once your momma left him, I fell in love with your daddy for the man he was. Even Huntington's could never take those memories away from me." She sipped the coffee he'd poured for her. "Aside from his pride, your father was a kind and generous man with a sense of humor like none other. Except maybe his son."

Her tender smile pierced Will's heart and he realized the depth of Rose O'Shea's love for his father. "Rose, Rose. I had no idea." He reached out to clasp her hands. "Why didn't I know? Was I that oblivious back then?"

Rose laughed. "Love isn't always about hugging and kissing and such. Sometimes it's simply the pure connection of two souls, two hearts and two minds."

He paused and considered her words. "I'm sorry, Rose."

"Don't be. As I said, I have my memories. Your father loved me. He told me many times. I had the confidence of at least knowing that. But he wouldn't hear of us getting married. Refused to do that to me, he said. In fact, more than once he told me I should leave." She paused and stared out the window into the dark morning. "Fortunately, Sullivans don't have a leg up on the O'Sheas when it comes to stubbornness. I flat out refused to leave."

Will gave a half smile. All these years he'd wondered what kept Rose at the ranch. He'd known it was love, known she loved him like a son, but he never suspected she loved his father as well.

Rose O'Shea could have been Rose Sullivan if his father had married her. As he held her hands and looked deep in her eyes, it sank in. While he understood his father's decision he regretted the loss. He already loved Rose as a mother. She deserved his father's name.

"I can understand why, Rose. He loved you and he wanted to spare you."

"Spare me? Will, was I going anywhere? Love doesn't run when there's trouble. Love is forever."

"Rose, my own mother ran."

"That was her loss," she answered, refusing, as she always had, to utter a negative thing about his mother. Instead she flipped through her Bible. Her finger slid down the page that she'd turned to, finally stopping. "First Corinthians thirteen— love bears all things, believes all things, hopes all things, endures all things. Love never ends." She closed her Bible. "And love never fails."

Will hung his head against what he knew she was going to say.

"Don't do this to Annie. At the very least tell her about the Huntington's. Don't you dare let her leave this ranch thinking you never cared enough to tell her the truth. Never cared, period. Because that's exactly what she believes."

"Wouldn't it be best that way? Not to have her hope she can change things?"

"You aren't going to make her stop loving you."

"She loves me?" He blinked, afraid to believe the words could be true, terrified of the answer at the same time. "Are you sure?"

"Well, of course, any fool can see that. At least let her know *why* you won't return her love."

"But I *do* love her."

Will paused, surprised at what had so naturally slipped from his lips.

"I do love her," he repeated softly.

Suddenly everything became clear. This was what kept him awake all night.

The inability to deny his love for Annie Harris. Fear of letting her love him back.

Rose smiled. "First time you realized it, huh?"

He nodded, shaken by the admission.

"I remember when I realized I loved your father. It left me speechless. I had no intention of falling in love. Especially at my age." She laughed, then shook her head.

Falling in love?

Yeah, he had fallen. And he was still falling.

Will swallowed hard, running his hands through his damp hair. He clenched his fists against the emotion that slammed into him.

How had it happened? He'd guarded his heart for so long. Who else but Annie could have snuck past his defenses?

"I'm begging you not to repeat your father's

mistake. You are his son, but I believe you are also wiser with your years, Will."

"I'm not so sure." He gripped the mug, feeling unsteady.

The only thing he knew for certain was that he loved Annie and he was confused. "Rose, nothing has changed about Huntington's. It's ten years later but there still isn't a cure. I read about it constantly, hoping something will change. But it's the same words over and over. Sure, great, I take a test. Fifty percent chance of being negative. What about the other fifty percent? What did I read somewhere? That it still equals one hundred percent Huntington's."

"Will, you could die tomorrow. You could die next week. Your days are numbered of the Lord, not of Will Sullivan. Good night. Stop and think about it. We could have lost Annie in Africa."

He shuddered, knowing she was right and yet unable to let go.

"You're all backward. You're figuring each day as a death sentence instead of a gift."

"Rose, it's enough for me to carry this burden. I can't...won't...give it to Annie."

"Will, Will, you listen, but your ears are closed. The burden is the Lord's. Annie has more substance than you and I both. She can handle this."

He nodded numbly, his strength to argue fading fast.

Rose reached out to touch his arm. "What is faith, Will?"

His glance connected with hers and he wanted so

much to be able to see things her way, but he couldn't get past the pain of his father's last days and his own fear of tomorrow.

Rose gave him a sweet smile. "You have to let go before you can take the first step."

He thought he had made peace with the Huntington's. He thought he was walking with the Lord on this. Wasn't he?

"Can you at least tell Annie?" she persisted.

Will covered her hand with his and released a breath. "All right. Yes. You're right. She deserves that much." He paused and looked Rose in the eye. "But it won't change anything."

"We'll see." She closed her Bible. "When are you going to tell her?"

"When I have to."

Rose chuckled. "There you go. Spoken like a true Sullivan."

Will finished his chores and showered. He ducked his head into Annie's room. "Annie?" Her bed was made and her trunk was open. Packed but open. A thread of panic ran through him.

She was leaving already? Had he run out of time already?

Will headed Okie out of the yard, into the fields and toward the peach orchards.

Rose was right. Annie at least deserved to know about the Huntington's. She was a part of their family and it was plain wrong for her to be on the outside.

Good thing she was at the orchard. It was probably

the only private spot on the ranch. Lately he felt as if he was surrounded by people. There was noise everywhere he went except the corners of the ranch.

Picking up speed, he nudged the mare into a canter, praying he'd find the right words by the time he reached the orchard.

She'd parked the Jeep under an elm tree in the shade. Will brought Okie to a halt. He pulled the reins into his left hand, dropped the stirrups, and gently vaulted off the horse. Glancing around, he still didn't see Annie, so he tied the leather reins to the Jeep's fender.

He walked up and down the rows until finally spotting her denim-clad legs on a ladder in the middle of the last row of peach trees.

"Need some help?" he called.

"What did you have in mind? Eating or picking?"

"Either one."

She continued to pick the fruit, not stopping to glance down, but placing each ripe peach in a bushel balanced on the top seat of the ladder.

"These peaches are more than ready," he remarked idly, removing his gloves and reaching up to examine the fuzzy fruit that dangled on the branches. "Going to be busy this week, aren't we?"

"Lots of pies for you," she said.

"For me or for Ryan?" he asked.

"You're jealous Rose's sharing pies with Ryan?"

"You bet I am."

Annie laughed and the sound warmed him.

"You want to hand me that bushel?" he asked.

Eyes averted, she stepped down a rung and slid the basket from the top of the ladder. Her hands brushed his as she eased the load to his arms.

He stumbled back, dazed by the simple touch of her hand.

"Careful," Annie said. "Don't fall."

"Too late for that," he answered. "I'm already a goner."

She looked at him curiously. "What?"

"Nothing."

He lifted the bushel of fragrant fruit into the back of the Jeep. There was already a small basket of blackberries loaded. "I see you found the last of the blackberries."

"Not many."

"Enough for a couple pies, though, isn't it?" he said, popping a few of the rich berries into his mouth.

"Unless someone eats them all first."

Will glanced at her hands. "Are you talking about you or me?"

Red-faced, she tucked her berry-stained hands into her pockets. "I have no idea what you're talking about."

Will chuckled. "You're done picking?"

"For today."

Folding up the ladder, he arranged it onto the back of the Jeep, securing it with a length of rope. He turned to face her. "So do you mind clearing up something for me?"

"What would that be?" she asked, suspicion etching her face.

"When are you leaving?"

"I haven't decided yet. There are two slots open, and it depends on how fast I can get everything tied up."

"Then why is your trunk packed?"

"I never unpacked it."

"What? Why not?"

"I knew that Sullivan Ranch was only a stop on the way."

"On the way to what?"

She shrugged. "Whatever the Lord has planned for me."

"I see."

"You didn't come all the way out here to try to convince me I shouldn't go to Mexico, did you?"

"Me? Naw."

"Then maybe you're here to try to get me to hurry up and leave?"

"Annie, you know better. But I did want to apologize, if you'll let me."

She frowned. "Apologize for what?"

"Oh, I've got a whole list, if you've got a few minutes."

"You think a whole list is going to take a few minutes?"

"You going somewhere?"

"Eventually," she said.

Will narrowed his eyes.

"I've got some water bottles in the cooler in the front seat. Want one?" she asked.

Taking off his Stetson, he nodded and moved to a grassy spot in the shade. He let his riding gloves drop to the ground.

Tossing a bottle to him, Annie drank from hers, all the while watching him, her expression wary.

"Pull up a chair," Will said, settling on the grass.

She complied. Legs folded, she leaned back on her hands.

"I need to talk to you about my father."

Her eyes grew round.

"Annie, I've never really explained to you what happened. I've never told anyone for that matter. Except Rose."

"You don't have to do this, Will."

"I do. I've already wasted enough time." He plucked at the grass, wondering where to begin. A hot breeze blew past, ruffling Annie's hair.

"Are you okay?" she asked.

He nodded. "I told you my dad did die of pneumonia, but what I didn't say is that it was a complication of his disease."

Annie said nothing, simply waited on him.

Will cleared his throat and unscrewed the cap of the water bottle, taking a long swig. "The other thing I never told you is that my father had Huntington's chorea, Huntington's disease. Whatever you want to call it."

"Dear Lord," she gasped, sitting up straight. Her

gaze remained fixed on him. Confusion and pain moved across her face. But never once what he'd feared most. Pity.

"My grandfather was adopted." He fiddled with the label on the bottle, peeling the paper as he spoke. "My dad is the first one I know of who has developed the disease. I've talked to the doctors and read all the literature. Bottom line never changes." He rubbed a hand over his mouth. "I, uh, I can count on a fifty-fifty chance of carrying the gene for Huntington's."

He paused, collecting his thoughts.

"So that's why you have a card from a neurologist in the Jeep."

"You saw that? Well, yeah. Dr. Nolan. He was my father's doctor, too."

"Why didn't you tell me?"

"My mother divorced my dad when he started having symptoms. She couldn't handle a sick husband. It's always been safer not to tell anyone."

"I'm not like your mother."

"I know. And I'm sorry I never told you." Relief washed over him.

"Why did you feel the need to carry this by yourself all this time?"

"Rose calls it Sullivan stubbornness." He shrugged.

"I guess she nailed you, did she?"

A half smile escaped from his lips at her words.

"Haven't they isolated the gene?" Annie asked.

"Yeah. I can be tested. A test will tell me if I carry

the gene. If I do I will develop Huntington's. When and how severe is a question that no one can answer. Up until now I just haven't seen the point in looking for trouble."

"I see."

"Annie, there's something else."

She raised a brow.

He took a deep breath. "About that night."

A long silence ensued.

"Consider it forgotten." She turned her head away in a gesture of dismissal. "It was just a kiss."

"No," he said, his voice getting louder. "I can't forget about it. That's the problem. I wish I could."

He heard her small gasp and when she turned back toward him, her face was a mixture of stunned surprise at his outburst.

Fact was, even he was a little surprised at his outburst. When she began to blink over and over again he began to worry.

Now it was his turn to ask. "You okay?"

Annie opened her hands and closed them.

"I don't know what to do about it, Annie."

"I can see how this might be a real problem for you, Will." She took a deep breath. "I never meant to be part of anything that would, well, that could threaten the ranch."

"Who told you that?"

"I overheard Margaret. I wasn't eavesdropping, I was just there."

Will gritted his teeth for a moment, angry that Margaret had cause Annie pain. "No. You don't get it. I don't want to forget it. That kiss meant something to me. It meant everything to me."

He stared up through the dense branches of the elm tree searching for the right words. "Look, I wasn't going to say anything. Rose insisted I tell you."

"You wouldn't have?" Eyes sparking, her voice jumped an octave and her cheekbones became splotchy and red with emotion.

Uh-oh. There was no mistaking the signs now. *Mad.*

Annie was mad as all get-out.

"No. After what I told you about my dad, you have to see that I have more than a chance of Huntington's. What kind of thing is that to lay on you?"

"Let me get this straight. You're telling me all this because Rose made you?"

"Well, yeah, basically."

"So if not for Rose, you would have let me go again. Never told me—anything?"

"I wouldn't have told you because I care for you."

"Please."

His head snapped back at her sarcasm. "Excuse me?"

"You heard me," she continued. "Tell me, Will, I'm curious. What did the Lord have to say on the subject?"

"Leave the Lord out of this. He and I have an understanding."

"Oh, I bet you do. You run the show. The Will show."

Will stared at her. What was going on? He never in a million years expected this turn in the conversation.

"Hold on here, just a minute." He rolled to his knees and stood. Pacing back and forth, he tried to figure out exactly what had just transpired. He glanced down at where she still sat on the grass.

"Annie, why are you leaving?"

"Because I did overhear your conversation with Margaret, and I won't do anything to threaten Sullivan Ranch. Besides, it's time to get on with my life."

"Margaret was barking up the wrong tree." He met Annie's dark eyes, straight on. "Do you have feelings for me?"

"Feelings?" In a heartbeat her lower lip began to tremble and a hot tear slipped from the corner of her eye.

"Awe, what are you doing? Anne E. doesn't cry."

"I am not crying." She swiped at her face with the back of her hand.

Will knelt down in front of her. "I am so lousy at this stuff. Jones never would have made you cry."

"I don't love Ryan. I love you, Will."

"You do?" His heart soared then crash-landed. "That's what I was afraid of." He leaned his forehead against hers. "What are we going to do about this situation?"

She sniffed again.

"Now what are you crying for?" he asked, getting more and more nervous by the second.

"I am not crying!"

"Well, you're looking mighty emotional to me."

"What do you expect? I tell you I love you and then you ask me what we're going to do about it, as though it was the worst thing that ever happened to you."

"No. Trust me, this isn't nearly close to the worst thing that ever happened to me."

Annie's face screwed up in surprise and confusion.

"That's not what I meant. Ah, Annie," he sighed, smoothing her mane of dark hair back with his hands. "Only the Lord knows how much I love you."

She lifted her face to his, hope lighting up her eyes.

Will placed a small kiss on each of her brows.

He leaned closer. When his lips touched hers for a tender kiss, the world rocked in its orbit. Putting her away from him, he took a deep breath. "I suppose if I had the genetic testing, then maybe we could talk about the future."

Annie sucked in a gulp of air. "Will Sullivan, you just don't get it, do you?"

"What did I do now?"

This time it was Annie who stood, hands on hips. "My love for you is not based on the results of a test."

"That's easy to say, but I saw what happened to my father. I watched my mother walk away."

"Did you leave him? Did Rose leave?"

"No, of course not."

"I love you. Think about what that means."

"No need to get bent out of shape here. I'm only thinking of you."

"You're giving me an out."

"Well, yeah." He gestured with his hands.

"I don't want an out. I want unconditional love from you and I want it forever. Those are my only terms. Nonnegotiable."

"What are you saying?"

"I'm saying that I don't want you tested."

Will stared, unable to comprehend. Those were the last words he expected from Annie.

"I'm a nurse, Will. I understand Huntington's. I understand the implications for the future."

He eased from his haunches and stood. "Do you understand that it means putting someone I care about through the possible torture of watching me die a little every single day?"

"I understand all of that. I told you once you're an all-or-nothing guy. Well, maybe you need to realize I'm an all-or-nothing woman. I don't want to be offered marriage based on any test results. I want you to ask me to marry you because you know that I am God's best for you—because you love me and can't live without me. Period."

"I can't do that."

"Why?"

"Annie, I can't offer you marriage when I don't know what my future holds."

"Does anyone know what the future holds?"

He paced back and forth across the grass. "You know what I mean."

"Are you willing to let me go through the torture of dying a little every day because I can't be with the man I love?"

"Now you're twisting my words around."

"Am I?"

Will kicked the ground. "What about children?"

"Children? Oh, for goodness' sake. What about them? Do you have to have all your *i*'s dotted now? My love for you is not based on having children."

"I love you, Annie. It scares me how fast and how hard this love for you has hit me. But marriage? That's something else."

Finger pointed, she walked up to him and poked him in the chest. "Will Sullivan. It's time to admit you're afraid. Time to admit it and make yourself vulnerable to what God wants for you."

"That's not the issue here. I said I'd take the test, didn't I?"

"This isn't about having the courage to take a test. It's about having the faith to give yourself to God. Until you can accept His unconditional love, you won't be able to accept mine."

"That's a bag of nails."

"Excuse me?"

"Annie—"

"No." She turned away and crossed her arms over

her chest, obviously unwilling to hear more. "As far as I can see I'm right back where I started. In love with a man who doesn't return my feelings. Mexico is sounding better and better."

"Forget Mexico."

She glared at him.

"Annie—"

"When you're ready to give up control, when you're ready for my love without your terms and conditions, let me know." She dug in her pocket and pulled out keys. "The one thing you aren't getting through your thick cowboy head is that I love you. I always will."

He couldn't believe this was happening. "But—"

"But nothing. What you have done is sentence us both to life without love because of your stubborn Sullivan pride." She crossed to the Jeep. "I can see it's a darn good thing I didn't unpack."

Untying the reins from the bumper, she handed them to him and calmly got into the Jeep. The engine roared followed by a loud scraping noise as the reverse gear jammed.

Will grimaced. "Uh, that's Third, not Reverse."

"Thank you," Annie said, smiling sweetly, her eyes sparking with unleashed anger. She shoved the clutch into Reverse.

Annie started counting as she watched the green trees of the orchard from the Jeep's rearview mirror. Will had paced back and forth half a dozen times and now appeared to be talking to Okie.

"One," she said aloud. "Lord, he needs to be talking to You, not that silly horse."

She checked the mirror again and slowed down the Jeep, shoving it into second gear. There was no use getting ahead of herself. Men were slower at things than women. She let the vehicle coast a bit.

Shaking his head, Will jammed on his hat. In the next moment he tightened the cinch on the horse, mounted and now sat in the saddle under the peach trees, apparently thinking.

"Two," she said. "What's there to think about? That cowboy is running out of time." She put her foot on the gas. "And I am running out of sweet patience. I'll be crossing the border into Mexico before he figures it out he really loves me."

A moment later Will, astride Okie, was next to the Jeep motioning for her to stop.

"I can't hear you," she called.

"Pull over," he hollered, irritation rising in his voice.

"What?"

"I said pull over, Annie."

"Three," she announced, slowing down to a stop and jerking up the parking brake.

"What did you say?"

"I said three."

"You were counting?" His blue eyes widened with realization.

"You bet I was. That was close. You almost ran out of time."

He removed his hat and scratched his head, then

set the hat on the back of his head. "I swear I will never figure women out."

"You don't need to. Just concentrate on me. I'll keep you busy for the next hundred years or so."

He swung off Okie, walked over to the Jeep and, hands on the roof, stared at her for several moments.

Finally he leaned into the vehicle, and for the longest moment his gaze simply met hers.

"I'm scared, Annie."

"I know, Will. I know." She blinked back the moisture pricking at her eyes.

"No, Annie. I don't think you do. I'm not just scared. I'm terrified."

"I do understand, because that's exactly how I feel. Terrified you're going to give up on us."

"You know, I always thought my greatest fear was the Huntington's." He released a ragged breath as though her confession had freed him. "I was wrong. Seeing you drive off, I realized that you leaving again is my greatest fear."

"Will," Annie breathed.

"I realized I have prayed every day for the past two years for you to come back. Oh, not your kind of prayer, but prayers nonetheless."

"He heard you. He always hears you."

"I guess so."

"And the past six weeks all I've done is pray for a way to make you stay. Apparently all I had to do was love you."

She smiled, biting back the emotions pouring into her heart.

"We'll do it your way, Annie," he said, his voice husky.

"No, Will, we do it God's way. We turn it all over to Him. Day by day, moment by moment. For the rest of our lives."

He nodded solemnly, his eyes bright.

"When it's time, then you'll take the test. But it won't change our love, because we are forever."

"Forever," he repeated the words with reverence, his lips a gentle caress against hers. "I never thought forever was something I'd hold in my hands."

She smiled tenderly at this man she loved so much.

"You are so beautiful," he said.

Annie felt the heat rise in her cheeks.

"What was that verse about love, the one that Rose talks about?"

"Love never fails."

He nodded. "I love you, Annie."

This time she kissed him with all the love she'd been saving for God's best. Annie gasped at the sweet beauty of his lips on hers.

Finally and much to her regret he released her.

"Now that is what we should be doing, instead of arguing."

"Not until after the wedding."

Will grinned. "Does this mean you're going to keep helping me with the ranch? 'Cause you know, between us, I'm thinking we're going to turn that ranch into our legacy."

"You'll have to hire me full-time, you know."

"So you're not going to Mexico?"

"Maybe for a honeymoon?" she countered.

Will's eyes lit up and he smiled. "As long as we always come home to Sullivan Ranch."

Epilogue

The opening chords of Pachelbel's "Canon" began, and Will watched as the barn door slowly opened and the small processional began.

The rafters twinkled with thousands of tiny golden lights, lending an ethereal glow to the converted barn. Bouquets of chrysanthemums, daisies and brown-eyed Susans overflowed from baskets that led from the barn door to the platform in back where Will, Ryan and Pastor Jameson waited.

Wedding attendants, Chris LaFarge and his wife, Joanie, slowly moved up the aisle, followed by Lulu Parson. Today Lulu had given up her usual polka dots for the simple cranberry matron-of-honor dress that matched the autumn flowers Annie had chosen for the wedding.

Annie was right as usual. The barn was the perfect setting for a wedding. Their wedding.

"So how's it feel to be the luckiest guy in the world?"

Will turned slightly to catch the expression on Ryan Jones's face, his attention never leaving the door where his bride would soon appear.

"You know, Doc, I only asked you to be best man so I could keep an eye on you."

Jones laughed. "No worries. Annie loves you, so I've decided that's good enough for me. And I guess you're not so bad if you like the silent, cranky type."

"Who's that you brought to the wedding?" Will looked out at the guests seated on the satin-covered folding chairs. There was a dark haired woman behind Rose's sister, but her face was obstructed by Ellen's straw-brimmed hat.

Suddenly the music transitioned and bold notes of Mendelssohn's "Wedding March" filled the large building, echoing to the ceiling.

"We'll talk later, Hoss," Ryan said. "I believe this is the moment you've been waiting for."

Will blinked as Annie stood in the doorway like a princess in frothy white, her hair long and flowing with small flowers at the crown of her veil. The light behind her blinded him for a moment until she stepped onto the carpeted runner.

Then there she was. *Annie.* She never looked more beautiful. It was only right that it was Rose who escorted the bride to her groom.

The picture left Will breathless, his heart full.

He swayed.

"You okay?" Ryan whispered.

Annie smiled at him from beneath the sheer veil, and Will nodded.

The hardest thing he'd ever done was to let God in and let Annie love him back. *Yeah, he was going to be okay.*

* * * * *

Dear Reader,

I hope you enjoyed my very first Love Inspired Inspirational Romance. I am delighted to be able to share Will and Annie's story with you. I lived seventeen years in Oklahoma, working most of that time as a registered nurse. Granby, Oklahoma, is a fictitious town but was created using my wonderful memories of all those great towns I lived near, such as Bixby and Jenks. I have a very special niece who told me once that God gives us grace for one day at a time. That's very much the heart of *The Rancher's Reunion*. Both Annie and Will must learn just as we must, to trust the Lord one step at a time. Thank you for reading their story. I would love to hear from you. You can reach me at my website, www.tinaradcliffe. com or by email at tina@tinaradcliffe.com.

Tina Radcliffe

QUESTIONS FOR DISCUSSION

1. One theme of *The Rancher's Reunion* involves living today and letting God take care of tomorrow. That's a difficult thing to do. How are you able to incorporate this theme into your life?

2. Will admits that he follows God on his terms. Do you have areas where you struggle to let go and let God?

3. Annie Harris dealt with survivor's guilt because she was alive after the attack on the clinic. Have you ever known someone who also dealt with survivor's guilt? Were they able to turn it over to God for the ultimate healing?

4. Annie, Will and Rose are not biological family but they feel like they are. Can you relate to this? Is there anyone in your life who, while not really your family, shares a special bond with you that is like family?

5. The setting for this book is a small town outside of Tulsa, Oklahoma. Small towns often have a unique and special community feeling. What are the small towns you are familiar with, and how do they evoke community?

6. Annie and Ryan discuss the pastor's sermon for the singles group, about waiting for God's

best for their life. What are your thoughts on singles finding God's best?

7. Will Sullivan carries a tremendous burden. Huntington's chorea, or Huntington's disease, has had a breakthrough with the isolation of the gene in 1993. Have you ever heard of this disease or ever known anyone who was diagnosed with this disease? More information can be found at the Huntington's Disease Society of America website, www.hdsa.org.

8. Annie struggles with concerns that she has some negative qualities that her mother had. What is your thought on this? Do you believe people can inherit character traits? If so, can God still free us from those negative traits?

9. Lulu and Howard reconnected late in life. Lulu sees beyond Howard's physical impairment. Have you ever known couples who reconnected in their golden years? Share some of these happy stories.

10. Will discovers that the symptoms he is having are stress-related, not the Huntington's. Have you ever gone through a period in your life when you were very stressed and ultimately that stress made you ill? If you can relate, how were you able to turn things around?

11. Margaret Reilly is a very savvy and sophisticated Christian businesswoman. She can also be very controlling. How can we deal in love with controlling people in our lives? How do we set boundaries?

12. Annie doesn't want Will to be tested yet. This is because she wants him to understand that her love, like God's, is unconditional. It is not based on a test and it will not change. What are your responses to Annie's request?

13. Who is your favorite character in *The Rancher's Reunion,* and why do you relate to them?

14. What is your favorite scene in this story? Why, and what emotions did it bring out?

15. Sullivan Ranch ties Annie, Will and Rose together. It is only fitting that Annie and Will marry at the ranch. What do you think of this setting for a wedding? Have you known other couples who chose settings that meant a lot to them yet were unusual places for a wedding?

LARGER-PRINT BOOKS!

GET 2 FREE LARGER-PRINT NOVELS PLUS 2 FREE MYSTERY GIFTS

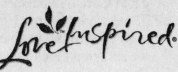

Larger-print novels are now available...

ReaderService.com

You can now manage your account online!

- Review your order history
- Manage your payments
- Update your address

We've redesigned the Reader Service website just for you.

Now you can:

- Read excerpts
- Respond to mailings and special monthly offers
- Learn about new series available to you

Visit us today:
www.ReaderService.com